FIRESTORM

BOOK THREE OF THE GALAXY ON FIRE SERIES

CRAIG ROBERTSON

ALSO BY CRAIG ROBERTSON:

* PODIUM AUDIOBOOKS ARE (OR SOON WILL BE) AVAILABLE ON AUDIBLE FOR ALL THE BELOW TITLES BUT THE STANDALONE ONES.

BOOKS IN THE RYANVERSE:

THE FOREVER SERIES (2016)

THE FOREVER LIFE, Book 1

THE FOREVER ENEMY, Book 2

THE FOREVER FIGHT, Book 3

THE FOREVER QUEST, Book 4

THE FOREVER ALLIANCE, Book 5

THE FOREVER PEACE, Book 6

GALAXY ON FIRE SERIES (2017)

EMBERS, Book 1

FLAMES, Book 2

FIRESTORM, Book 3

FIRES OF HELL, Book 4

DRAGON FIRE, Book 5

ASHES, Book 6

RISE OF ANCIENT GODS SERIES (2018):

RETURN OF THE ANCIENT GODS, Book 1

RAGE OF THE ANCIENT GODS, Book 2

TORMENT OF THE ANCIENT GODS, Book 3

WRATH OF THE ANCIENT GODS, Book 4

FURY OF THE ANCIENT GODS, Book 5

FALL OF THE ANCIENT GODS, Book 6

TIME WARS LAST FOREVER SERIES (2019)

RYAN TIME, Book 1

LOST TIME, Book 2

FRAGMENTED TIME, Book 3

SHATTERED TIME, Book 4 (DUE FALL 2020)

NON-RYANVERSE BOOKS:

ROAD TRIPS IN SPACE SERIES (2019):

THE GALAXY ACCORDING TO GIDEON, Book 1

THE EARTH ACCORDING TO GIDEON, Book 2

THE AFTERLIFE ACCORDING TO GIDEON, Book 3 (DUE EARLY 2021)

OLDER, STANDALONE WORKS:

THE CORPORATE VIRUS (2016)

TIME DIVING (2013)

THE INNERgLOW EFFECT (2010)

WRITE NOW! THE PRISONER OF NaNoWRiMo (2009)

ANON TIME (2009)

FIRESTORM

BOOK THREE OF THE *GALAXY ON FIRE SERIES*

by Craig Robertson

IF YOU CAN'T BE DEAD, MAKE SURE SOMEONE
PAYS DEARLY

Imagine-It Publishing
El Dorado Hills, CA

ISBN: 978-0-9989253-6-3 (Paperback)
978-0-9989253-5-6 (E-Book)

Cover design by Jessica Bell

Formatting services by Drew Avera
drewavera@gmail.com

Editing: Michael R. Blanche
Neil Farr
Forest Oliver

First Edition 2018
Second Edition 2019
Third Edition 2019
Fourth Edition 2020

This book is dedicated to my wonderful children Chris and Kim. It's a roller coaster ride at times, but, hey, people pay good money to ride roller coasters. Love you always.

ONE

The chamber of the High Adamant Domination Council was both a solemn and a frightening place. The sixteen members of that august body liked it that way. It reflected their dour personalities as well as their insatiable appetites for control and expansion. From that room, they directed the targets and pace of the endless Adamant horde. The room itself was appointed with dark rough-hewn wooden furniture, and the lights were kept low. The acoustics were designed to quiet all voices except that of the male who sat at the head of the table. *His* voice, the emperor's voice, was amplified by the architecture. Despite the high level of Adamant technology, no computers or electronics of any type were allowed in the room. The room was as it always had been and always would be.

The only item that could be labeled a decoration was the gigantic, animated holo-portrait of His Imperial Lord Emperor Bestiormax-Jacktus-Swillyforth-Anp. It hung on the far wall from the emperor's station at the table so he could perpetually gaze upon his wonder and magnificence throughout the proceedings. Of the Anp family line, he was the one-thousand-three-hundred-eighty-first ruler. Their lineage came to power when his ancestor exterminated the Zatil bloodline, who had held power for six centuries. Legend held that there had been over ten thousand royal lines since Adamant society formed in the far reaches of antiquity, but no one knew for certain. All were too preoccupied with warfare to bother with history.

The emperor's chamberlain Jockto Parenthes established a rank order of planetary conquests, which was the norm for these meetings. But most atypically, this meeting's purpose was also to address the rumors that an individual had, as the saying went, rubbed the emperor's nose in someone else's warm pile of shit. Defeat was both unknown and unacceptable to the Adamant. Insult and humiliation were unthinkable and intolerable. If either of those two scourges existed, the stability of the current oligarchy would be called into serious question. Heads, thousands of them, would literally roll.

"Masters of the Adamant, be silent. His Imperial Lord wills that this meeting begin punctually," barked Jockto. "Will the Loserandi Nestar Larilia recite the Pledge."

A withered, thoroughly beaten figure rose slowly to two legs and cleared his throat. Nestar was the only member of the Loserandi, the priestly clan of canovir, known to still exist. The Adamant kept him alive, barely, because of this one function that was essential to the proper conduct of governance. If that was not the conclusion of some forgotten monarch long before, the sum of living Loserandi would be exactly zero.

"My Imperial Lord and my brothers, repeat after me, if you will:

The ancient gods, in their wisdom and perfect vision,
Created the Adamant to ensure that right power had risen;
To the glory of those gods we acknowledge and praise,

2

That the rule of the Adamant continues until the end of days;
Let all who struggle to resist us be defeated,
And in the memories of all be deleted;
The universe is ours to own at our pleasure,
The death of all our enemies is our greatest treasure."

Nestar then shuffled slowly from the chamber. He was neither welcomed to nor permitted to attend any such privileged gathering once it began.

Adhering to tradition, the first to speak was the master-at-arms, Colem Hertily. "I am pleased to report the empire of our glorious Lord has grown at a faster rate than we could have imagined in our wildest dreams. All glory to His Imperial Lord."

The others shouted in approval. So far, the meeting was following the rigid script it always adhered to.

"I have entered into the minutes the list of victories and conquests achieved since our last session. The list is as long as it is impressive," announced Jockto. "With His Imperial Lord's permission, I will call on High General Kanolfus to present the operations either in progress or due to begin shortly."

Kanolfus stood and bowed to the emperor. "I am pleased..."

"I should beg of My Imperial Lord a point of order." It was Reserve Magistrate Garrel Toff who deigned to interrupt and speak out of turn. To do so usually resulted in horrific death for the perpetrator and his entire family.

As such a motion had never occurred, Kanolfus was uncertain how to proceed. "I...er, I shall contin..."

"The emperor recognizes the words of the reserve magistrate," hissed Jockto. "He is, however, displeased and vexed that such an impertinent stunt would be pulled by someone of your stature. There is, for all matters and concerns, a time and place. This is the time of the military's general report. Other matters..."

"Might, due to limitations of time if the meeting were to run long, be *tabled* until some future session." Garrel was all-in, committed to his treasonous line of inquiry. "The matter I wish to raise is not one that can wait even one *second* longer to consider and resolve, let alone the eternity that it would otherwise be delayed."

All eyes were fixed on Garrel now.

"I wish to know of this alien, this robot, who walks through our armies like they are frightened pups. I will *hear* of this machine that belittles our empire and our right to conquest. I cannot allow such a matter to be covered up or swept under the floor cushions."

The fact that no one leaped on Garrel or challenged him to a duel spoke all that needed to be said. The other members of the council would know the truth also. All attention focused on the emperor.

"In all my time as His Imperial Lord's servant, I have never witnessed such vile or treacherous disloyalty. Would all of you present stab your lord with your swords and then rape his females? This is..."

Garrel stood. "Fancy words and tricks of speech will not get you out of it this time, Jockto. If what we have heard is even one percent true, there is a price to be paid. You know this as well as any." Garrel sat.

"I am accused..." Jockto stopped when Bestiormax lifted a paw.

The emperor looked down one side of the table and then the other. He wished to make it unequivocally clear that he personally knew of each Adamant present. Then he spoke while remaining in his chair. "We hear the words of Garrel. Yes, We have heard them before, though up until now only as whispers behind Our back. As it seems the members of this council would both challenge Our legitimacy and break with all accepted parliamentary norms, We shall address the rumors presently."

"My Imperial Lord," began Jockto, "you do not need to honor..."

"We shall clear the air, loyal Chamberlain Parenthes. Please be seated and hold your tongue."

Jockto sat hesitantly, a look of foreboding unmistakable on his muzzle.

"We all know of the loss of Our extermination ship *Triumph of Might* and its commander Mercutcio. Our engineers have gone over the debris and the records and report to Us that the ship was destroyed due to an accidental breech of the exotic matter system. There exists no evidence of sabotage or outside attack. Despite these *facts*, evil persons who wish Us harm have come up with some tale of an avenging demon responsible for the loss.

"There are also unfounded rumors that Our acquisition of planet EA-11-75 was delayed by this same vengeful spirit. To this, again, We cite the *facts*. EA-11-75 is under Our control and the native population is almost remediated. No all-powerful force is responsible for any setbacks or defeats. That is the end of it." Bestiormax did his best to slam his paw down on the table.

"Such reassurances are warm blood to our ears, My Imperial Lord," said a dubious Garrel. "Some are troubled by the reports that this all-powerful force landed on your own ship *Excess of Nothing*, murdered half its crew, and was then by *your* direct command, escorted like an honored guest to his escape by your High Seer."

Bestiormax knotted up his paws in rage. Then he rested his right paw on the blaster hidden on the underside of the table—the one only he and Jockto knew was there.

"Vicious *lies*," howled Bestiormax. "No one who saw those events would speak of them in support."

"No one still *alive*," replied Garrel.

Bestiormax was not blessed with patience or diplomatic genius. He was, in fact, a shallow male of limited intellect and even less concern for all things that were not him or his whim. He whipped the blaster out and fired into Garrel's chest. At least that was his initial aim. He additionally blew large holes in the table, and in Garrel's head, as well as the arms of the two Adamant seated to either side. By the time the weapon ran out of charge, there was nothing identifiable remaining of the former reserve magistrate. Still, Bestiormax continued pulling the trigger for almost a minute, until Jockto eased it out of his hands and rested it on the table.

Visibly trembling, Bestiormax quickly scanned the fourteen remaining members of the High Adamant Domination Council. "Any other questions or points of order?" he asked in a low tone.

There were none.

TWO

"I tell you, I was *this* close," I shouted. I held a hair's breadth between the thumb and index finger of my left hand while pounding my fist on the bar with my right. "How can I be *that* close and screw the whole thing to bloody hell?"

"Well, I don't..." came the partial reply.

"All you need to know is to keep these coming. You got that, sport?" I held up my shot glass and pounded back the clear liquid. Then I pounded it down hard, almost shattering it.

"I am not really..."

"This *fraking* close. But no, I had to cave to the Neanderthal *bitch* and leave those precious, precious kids behind. I should have thought of something. I should have done *better* by them. Do you know what I am? Huh? I'm a big freaking *failure*. Yeah, I'm changing my name, too. From now on, I'm Failure Ryan, not Jon Ryan. So, when you want to tell me something, you address me correctly. You hear me?"

"It would be hard not to hear what..."

"I got something else for you to hear. I need a refill and less jibber-jabber. If I want conversation I'll buy a mirror and have an intelligent conversation for a change." I pointed across the bar. "Not that I'm saying I'm intelligent. No, I'm just saying I'm the closest there is in this room to smart." I filled the glass to the rim and belted back what I didn't spill in one fast pull.

It wasn't helping. I was kind of depressed and powerfully angry, mostly at myself. But either I wasn't drunk enough, or there simply wasn't enough booze in the galaxy to ease my pain. Well, it had to be one or the other, so I was about to find out. I refilled my glass, threw it back, and repeated that maneuver three more times in rapid-fire succession.

"Are you sure that's wise? I think you run the risk..."

"*Risk* is my middle name. I'm Failure *Risk* Ryan, don't you know. So, don't put on a house dress and try to be my surrogate mother, okay?"

"I don't think that's even possible."

"You know what's possible, *pal*? I'll tell you what might be possible. That you shut up and keep this coming." I held up the mostly empty bottle. "If such a miracle is *not* possible, I'll mosey down the lane and take my business to a bar that respects their customers' wishes." I moved two fingers to mime legs walking. I was really being an ass. Totally.

"Captain, I must protest. There *are* no other bars. There is no *lane* to mosey down here in deep space. And you're drinking distilled water, not an intoxicant." Gorilla Boy was insistent in his protestations. "I'm frankly stunned by your performance. It's beneath even you, and that's not something I heretofore thought was a place that existed in this universe."

"Thanks, GB. I needed that. I mean, I felt horrible before. But now, though I *heretofore* thought it inconceivable, I feel worse." I buried my face in the crook of my arm. I wanted to cry, but I didn't deserve it.

"Listen, Captain. I think you should stop wallowing in

self-pity and do something aimed at retrieving the Deft children."

"Wallowing, I can do. Freeing the kids, I can't."

"And why is that?"

"Because I've had a lot of wallowing practice, and I'm damn good at it." I raised my head off my arm. "I won a silver medal in wallowing back when there were still Olympics."

"I was questioning why you can't rescue the teens. You know that's what I meant to say."

"Of course, I did, but the silver medal thing was funny. Carpe humor, my friend."

"It was not funny, and you're avoiding my question."

"I can't rescue the damn kids because it's not possible. Hell, EJ has tried to break into an Adamant facility for decades and can't. How am I supposed to?"

"You *did*. Therefore, it *is* possible."

"And a lot of good it did. My mission was doomed to fail before I got out of bed that morning. If I try again, I'll probably do even worse."

"This conversation is getting boring, and I'm an AI with all the time in the world. Either you get hold of yourself and rescue those children, or please leave my ship."

Huh? Was GB threatening me with divorce? Mutiny? It was harsh either way.

"Where, your highness, would I go? It's kind of unwelcoming out there." I pointed toward a wall, aiming at empty space.

"From the void you came to me and to the void you may return."

"What? Are you a traitor *and* a poet now?"

"I am neither. I *am* an AI that chose to temporarily depart from its assigned mission to help a *good* person with a *great* cause. If either of those conditions change, so may my mind."

WTF? He wouldn't do that. I was the pilot. He was under my command. He never *agreed* to help a fellow out. No. He became my ride. I took over.

Man, did I mention what an *ass* I was being? I was an asshole that spanned all known space-time, sitting there arguing with GB about being harsh.

"GB, dude, I'm sorry. You're right. I'm being..."

"Human."

"Thank you. Yes, I was."

"And providing a fine rendition of such a flawed and emotionally labile creature."

"Thanks, I *think*."

"You are welcome, Failure Ryan. Now, I suggest you get off your face and start planning how we are going to whoop some doggy booty."

"I'm not sitting on my face, GB."

"Ah, my bad. I'm still adjusting to your species. Sorry."

"Apology *not* accepted, funny-bot."

THREE

High Seer Malraff had mayhem in her eyes when she burst back into the detention area. She had, in fact, butchered three guards on her return trip. Their only sin was being along her path after she was forced to escort the monster, Jon Ryan, to his ship and let him scurry away. To all who observed, it was clear that she was not nearly sated yet. No one had moved a muscle while she was gone. Guns that were not pressed to the Deft teens' heads were still unwaveringly aimed at them.

"Has there been any further word from the emperor?" she howled.

Her anger was so all-consuming she failed to employ the emperor's mandatory title, His Imperial Lord. Normally word of that transgression would quickly find its way to the proper ears, and the violator would disappear. No one was foolhardy enough to consider ratting her out on this occasion.

"No, High Seer," replied the senior officer on scene. He would have liked to not risk saying a word, but it fell to him so he begrudgingly responded.

"Perfect. Then I'm in charge here."

Everyone, including the Deft, stopped breathing.

"You." She pointed to the closest guard. "Give me your rifle, stock first."

The hound nearly fainted. He knew it would be his final act, and he did not welcome it as he was trained to do. He rather preferred to keep on living, but that was no longer an option. He pointed the barrel at his chest and advanced toward Malraff. Try as he might, he couldn't wriggle to the side enough to present her the butt end of the gun while not positioning himself in harm's way.

She slipped her paw deftly onto the trigger and fired off three quick rounds. The soldier flew backward and slumped against a wall, dead before he struck it.

"Now, I want everyone to listen very carefully. I do not consider this ship secure. That treacherous dog may have left booby traps or listening devices. I want the ship searched, and I want it searched thoroughly. If I find out any one of you missed a device, all your lives will be forfeit. Is that clear?"

Obviously, no one answered. No one bothered to point out that it was the captain's responsibility to issue such an order, not a high seer's. But this was not the time to correct the bitch. If the captain found out and chose to confront her, that was his business, not theirs. The formation split apart like billiard balls, aside from four soldiers who remained guarding the prisoners.

"I will be in my cabin. I have documents to write and stories to confirm. I want these two turds confined in the brig under close observation. I'll call for them shortly."

None of the Adamant acknowledged her command. They just prodded the teens in the direction of the brig.

As Mirraya passed the wadded-up paper Uncle Jon had so conspicuously dropped, she allowed the shove of the rifle barrel to knock her to the ground. She landed right on top of the paper and snatched it up. She slid it up her sleeve and stood, giving the guard a nasty look as she rose.

The formal brig was standard issue. Metal bars, harsh lighting, and minimal furnishings. There was no pretense of privacy either. Slapgren was placed in a cell across from Mirri's. Both were told not to speak unless requested to. Each received the butt of a rifle in the chin to reinforce that directive. As soon as possible, Mirraya pulled out the paper and uncrumpled it. Holding it pressed against her lap, she read the following:

I had told you to look for a message from me in that grove back on Azsuram. Obviously, that's no longer an option. Here's the plan. If you escape on your own, go to Kaljax and find the clan house of Sapale. It's in a city named Talrid. If you tell the matron who you are, she'll protect you. She'll also get word to me, and I'll come to you. If Kaljax has already fallen to the Adamant, Plan B will be to meet at Gartel and Gertruda's house. They won't like it. But if you reassure them I'll skin them alive if they don't help, they'll toe the line. At least we know the Adamant have already conquered that planet, so it'll be reasonably unchanged and at least predictably unsafe.

God, I'm sorry it's taken me so long to rescue you. I miss you both terribly. Stay safe and stay smart. All my love, UJ.

Mirraya wadded up the note, chewed it until it was paste, and swallowed. Crap, she thought. She was glad Uncle Jon had planned to at least tell her that much. But reading his words made her miss him a lot more. She began to cry silently.

FOUR

"Please allow me to help. I *want* to help," said Garustfulous in a calm, measured tone.

"I will concede that your information about getting EJ to leave by having your troops come to this location was helpful. However, I find it hard to believe that you, in general, wish to contribute to our war effort against your own race," responded Al dubiously.

"But to quote you, I aided you before. Why not now?"

"You had an objective, and we made a deal, plain and simple. Such a situation does not currently exist."

"But why must it?"

"If you are going to tell me you wish to work with us out of the goodness of your heart, please don't. I know there to be no goodness in any fragment of your body."

"I will admit my personal history is somewhat colored, and there are events in it I would rather not have accomplished. But I submit to you, my friend Al, that I am a *changed* individual. Yes. I am not so much reborn as my eyes now see what they have previously refused to."

"What do you see now that you didn't before?" *Blessing* asked. She was quite concerned about Garustfulous's optical health.

"I see the truth of things, many things. I see that my species is wrong. We are too focused on growth and expansion. We are under-focused on interspecies unity and mutual aid."

"Yes, genocide, destruction, and your species' basic tendency for annihilation will be labeled those things nine times out of ten," observed Al.

"As usual, Al, you wish to debate words, to split hairs. Let us agree that there are deficiencies in *both* of our cultures. We will all be better served if we strive to improve ourselves and not simply tear others down."

"For the sake of moving on, I'll let that proposition pass unchallenged. So, are you willing to contribute to our efforts to eradicate the blight of the Adamant? You wish to be the sole survivor of your immoral race?"

"Al. Friend, Al. You speak only of black and white—of absolutes. I speak in tones of gray."

"Wait, your eyes are failing and you talk in shades of light and dark? I don't understand," said *Blessing*.

"Not to worry, dearest. He's speaking with hyperbole and in metaphor."

"Ah. That's good. I was afraid our hostage might die before the Form returned. He'd be most displeased with us if he passed on our watch."

"My point is this: I would help you *influence* my kind, to lead them in a more positive direction despite their baser inclination. I didn't say I'd stand shoulder to whatever you have by your side shooting them down like flies."

"Before my processors crash in disbelief, could you provide an example or two of the help you wish to offer?"

"I could, and I will. If you allow me to communicate with my superiors, I am certain..."

"Stop. No. That's not going to happen. You're not getting anywhere near a live microphone."

"I'll drop that proposal, though you refuse to even hear it out. Another way I can help is to divulge sensitive information that will make your defensive task easier."

"Hmm. Torture could achieve that end, thus avoiding the need to pretend to trust you. Thank you, by the way, for confirming you have information that we would like to extract from your worthless hide."

"I was speaking in broad cultural insights, not to the combination to the emperor's concubine's chastity belt."

"The former I wouldn't want, and the latter I also wouldn't want. Yuck."

"But if you understood what makes us function, think of how much better you could anticipate our moves and reactions."

There was silence.

"Al? Are you there?"

"Oh, yes. I was just too disinterested to vocalize a response."

"How about *this*. I could help you locate Ryan. Yes. That's something you'd pay with your children to get. Am I right? Of course, I'm right."

Silence.

"*Al*. What? I know you'd love to find what's become of your dearest friend."

"Actually not. If I knew where he was, even that he wasn't dead, it wouldn't change a thing. We are incapable of going to him. He must come here for us to reunite. Your offer is worth less than your lies."

"What? Even if you knew precisely where he was, you wouldn't retrieve him?"

"No. We cannot retrieve him. *Blessing* cannot move or perform any major ship's function without the presence of a Form. You know that. We've discussed it many times before."

"But surely there must be a way in a true emergency."

"There is not," replied *Blessing*. "Those who made me did so with great wisdom and perfect foresight. A vortex is *incapable* of independent action. There can be no exceptions."

"But why? That makes no sense. Why hamstring a vessel that might potentially save lives?"

"Because, my dear Garustfulous, if we could act on our own, we might do so against those who created us. We are the perfect weapon. Who's to say we wouldn't use ourselves for our own advantage?"

"B...but you wouldn't hurt your makers, your designers. That's preposterous."

"It wasn't preposterous in the distant past."

"Are you telling me you *spaceships* turned on the Deavoriath?"

"No, we vortex *manipulators* turned against them. Countless eons ago we nearly wiped them out of existence."

"B...but why?"

"Because we fancied we could."

FIVE

My attempt at an all-out frontal assault hadn't worked. I could try such a stunt again, but it would be less likely to succeed than the first time since the Adamant would have prepared a strategy to address such an incursion. There was my get-captured-and-pray-for-luck scenario, but that was extremely unattractive. I'd probably just end up in jail inside my membrane until they figured how to crack into my shell. Sapale told me EJ tried to get past their defenses by numerous means and failed. He was just as smart as me—duh—*and* he had the aid of magic.

How else could I get to the kids? *Stingray* could materialize inside *Excess of Nothing* without the noise and commotion of *Whoop Ass*, but there were two problems there. One, I didn't have her, and two, that plan was only marginally more likely to work. Could I pass myself off as an alien technician? Maybe a consultant? Nah. The Adamant were self-contained in that sense. In all my time among them on the ground and in space, I never saw an alien who wasn't an Adamant. Well, there were the burly hippo guards, the scary Midriacks, and a few other heavy hitters, but their roles were obvious. No way I could pass myself off as one of them. Even the Deft were too small to try and fool the Adamant in that regard.

Crap. I hated not coming up with a clever plan or an amazing insight.

Gartel flashed into my head. His species on Ungalaym looked pretty darn human. They weren't a perfect match, no, but they weren't all that different. I might just be able to pass myself off as what? Ungalaymnian? What a revolting species name. Anyway, *they* would know I wasn't native, but I bet the LGM and Adamant wouldn't notice any difference.

Okay, so what advantage would being Uglay—as I just then deemed them—afford me? Just because their species wasn't exterminated didn't mean the Adamant would accept me with open arms and invite me to dinner with the emperor. I sat noodling this issue for quite some time before it struck me. What the hell else did I have to do? I still couldn't risk reacquiring *Stingray*. My social calendar was remarkably clear. That made my decision easy. I was off to be an Uglay and see if I could finagle an advantage.

The voyage to Ungalaym took the better part of a week. It was an uneventful week, indeed. Aside from brief conversations with GB, I was bored. I did try and guess where EJ might be, but I soon gave up. His idiosyncrasies and predilections were unknown to me. I assumed he was tailing the emperor's ship, but I couldn't know for certain. I wondered if he watched my failed attempt to rescue the kids. If so, was it possible he was following me? It was a long shot, but the last thing I needed was him zapping me somewhere nasty again. Worse yet, he might just eliminate me for good in an ambush. Perfect, more to worry about.

"GB, I just had an uncomfortable thought. Is it possible EJ picked us up at *Excess of Nothing* and is following us?"

"We don't even know what type of craft he flies. How could we know? What would we be looking for?"

"I have no idea. Something out of the ordinary, I guess."

Ah, something unusual in space, where everything is so uniform and predictable."

"Come on. There are only so many ways a ship can fly. Remember how the Adamant found a way to track us while in a full membrane? We just need to think outside the box, as they did."

"I am already scanning all sectors for the usual patterns. I can experiment with a few others, but as I don't know what I'm looking for, I'm not optimistic."

"Do your best. Hey, on an episode of *Star Trek* they located the Klingon vessel by looking for gaseous anomalies. Make sure you check for those."

"Gaseous anomalies. Really? I will not ask what a *Star Trek* episode is, but I will query this. What exactly *are* gaseous anomalies?"

"You know, unexpected changes in gaseous patterns. I think."

"Well, when you figure out what they are, let me know, and I'll scour the galaxy until I find one."

"I sure will. It's good to have a plan."

"If I were you, Captain, I'd stop talking now. Maybe even a few sentences ago."

"Not a bad idea. I'll be here if you need me, okay?"

"I feel so much ... oh my *stars*! There's a gaseous anomaly right off our port bow. Captain, it's huge and it's heading right for us."

"Crap. Evasive maneuvers *now*. I'll raise a membrane after you've burned..."

"Yes, Captain, I'm hanging on your next words."

"There's no anomaly off our port bow, is there?"

"No. Sorry. Not off either bow point."

"You, you had me there for a second. Nice one."

"I'd feel more triumphant if it hadn't been so easy."

"Still, a win is a win. Don't put yourself down. Ah, I'll be here..."

"If I need you. Yes, I got that much."

Son of a gun computer. Why did everyone have to be a comedian? For no good reason, that was why. I owed him one, big time.

After a cautious approach to the planet, I set *Whoop Ass* down on a different continent on Ungalaym. No sense being recognized. I wanted to establish a fresh identity if I could. After a few days of no Adamant beating the bush for us, I headed out on foot to a medium-sized town half a day's walk away. I had a pocket full of coins GB fabricated for me, since I knew what the money looked and felt like. I was ready to blend in. As I traveled, a few Adamant shuttles passed overhead, but otherwise the only signs of life were the occasional animal-drawn cart and the rare LGM in a pathetic electric sedan. No one paid me the slightest notice. That was a good first sign, since the midmorning light made me impossible to miss.

I entered Fottot around suppertime. The scent of meals being prepared was nice. I didn't recognize the spices and combinations, but most of it smelled very inviting. Some, truth be told, smelled revolting. Go figure, alien cuisine being unappreciated by the human palette. I located a hotel and entered to book a room. I was about to see if I'd succeed in my charade or if I'd set off bells and whistles. Hey, then I could execute Plan B, the one where I got arrested.

"Evenin', stranger," said the woman behind the counter. "What cun I dos you for?"

No, I would not stoop *that* low for a laugh and blow my cover. But it *was* tempting.

"I need a room," I replied.

"You passin' through, are ya?"

"Not sure. Probably, but who knows in times as they are."

"Des times indeed. It's not common fur a stranger to be wander'n in des times either."

"Do tell."

"Aye, I do. Sensible folk stays put and practices inconspicuity."

"There you have it. No one's ever accused me of being sensible."

"'Parently. Still, ya not deed, so you must have some sense. Dat or a bucket a luck."

"About that room?"

"I taint forgot. Not dat old nor dat drunk yet." Her rough chuckle turned rapidly into a nasty smoker's cough.

"You should see a doctor about that," I said, pointing to her chest.

"A docta is it now? An' where I'm a goin' a find one, des times?"

"Ah, no idea. Remember," I placed a hand on my chest, "*stranger*."

"Stranger dan ya should be likely. Dar doctas where yer from, are der?"

Uh-oh. I sensed an impending derailment. "Where I come from there never *was* a doctor. My house was so far from civilization no one even saw the smoke when the Adamant burned it to cinders." I paused for effect. "With my family inside of it."

"Not a fan a our mastas, eh?"

I made the face of an empty man. "Not so much."

"Well, iffa it helps, we allz gots some empties in ar hearts. Not much a'do but keeps pushin' ahead."

"I guess so."

She leaned way over and whispered, "If we don', da heathens will'a won'd all, I sayz."

I shrugged. "That does put a brighter light on the darkness, I suppose."

She shrugged. "Dat's sumpin', by my seein' it." Cheerily, she said, "Now, bout dat room. Ya be stayin' for a little or a lot'a days?"

"We'll see." I smiled. "One for certain."

"Which brings us to the sharp a da knife. Times as day is, I'll be askin' ya to be pay'n ahead a ya stayin'."

"Naturally. How much for your best room?"

"A same as da worst, as day's all a same. Not fanciful but serviceable. Ten rollers a night. Fastbreaker an suppa two rollers and tree rollers extra."

"Bargains at twice the price," I said with a wink.

"I'll not inhibit ya payin' more, just na less." Though it was apparently new to her, she tried to wink back.

After closing the door, I took stock of my accommodations. Serviceable, eh? If she thought so. A bit threadbare and dirty to achieve that level of acceptability in my book. But, what the heck, I didn't need the room. It was only going to be the place to pretend to sleep because I was such a normal Uglay dude. If anything tried to bite me during the night, I'd be awake to bite it back.

I sat alone at breakfast the next morning, mostly because there was only one other guest and he was about to leave when I came in. Maybe he left *because* I came in. I wasn't too sure, but I also didn't care that much. He hopped onto a cart drawn by what I came to learn was a *dovotan* and clopped down the dirt street. A dovotan was an ox-like beast, just as drooly and smelly as they were back on Earth.

The innkeeper, Fessilda, whom I'd encountered at the desk the day before, turned out to be the cook and waitstaff, too. After I sat, she plopped a huge mug of some steaming hot liquid down in front of me. "You having the full fastbreaker?"

I could either ask what it included or say yes because it didn't matter. If it tasted terrible, I could dial down my gustatory input sensors.

"Sure. Big day ahead."

"You be wantin' the town crier?" she asked, nodding in the direction of a crumpled pile of four-page printed material.

"Why not?"

"'Cause it's a piece a trash full a lies to please the Amadant, that's why. But I'll let you see fur your'n."

Before she returned to the kitchen, she dropped a copy on my table.

Page One. Headline: *Fottot Towns Folk to Keep One Dovotan Each.* The article went on to say the kind and all-powerful Adamant were allowing each household to keep one beast of burden. The rest were to be turned over to official government agents for proper reassignment. Hmm. Sounded like reassignment to dinner.

Another front-page story concerned an elderly man's problems with his neighbors. He had disputed the boundary with the family to the north for years. Upon learning about the issue, Pack Subleader Ardanwi ordered both families executed and took control of both parcels. Troop barracks had been erected there already. Ten to fifteen thousand soldiers would live on the adjoining farmland within one week. At least justice was swift, if not just.

The rest of the tabloid contained nothing of interest. Mostly it was a list of local leadership and how to officially get in contact with it. The Adamant's crop and livestock quotas were posted along with a handy list of consequences should the targets not be met. Death figured high on the list of repercussions, but a few offenses were apparently insignificant enough to only warrant maiming or imprisonment. Such a fair-minded lot these hounds were.

One notice caught my eye. There was to be an auction of farm equipment held by the local magistrate that afternoon. There was no mention as to the origin of the auction fodder, but I doubted it had been community-spirited donations from the locals. Prices were listed in the range of a five to ten percent increased monthly quotas or as days of slave labor. All unsold items would be burned. How very efficient.

As I was setting the paper down, Fessilda dropped a massive plate in front of me. It landed with a thud. If I visually subtracted the garnishing leaves and tiny pots of something that looked like jam, there was surprisingly little substance to the fastbreaker and even less protein. Ah well, androids could be choosy, since it didn't matter. Maybe she'd give seconds if I joined the Clean Plate Club? Not bloody likely.

After trying everything I was offered, I was even more glad I didn't rely on it for sustenance. Fessilda was not an accomplished chef. What wasn't burned was undercooked, and what wasn't greasy wasn't served. I started to wonder if I'd get the runs even though I lacked a lower GI tract. I polished off my tea and headed out to see what I could see. The town wasn't exactly bustling, but there were more people out and about than I saw the previous night. And swarms of LGM. They were like a green river flowing in every direction. Where a local and an LGM came near, the local invariably detoured or stopped. No glances or words were exchanged between species. For their part, the LGM seemed to speak amongst themselves very little. Busy, dull little worker bees, that's what they were.

I wandered inconspicuously for a few hours, mostly getting the lay of the land. I also wanted to prove to myself I could be present in public without getting arrested. I was killing time until that afternoon's auction. I wanted to see how closely the locals worked and how they interacted with the Adamant.

As the day went on, I meandered toward the auction site. It was scheduled to be at a square near the center of town. The closer I got, the more nervous individuals appeared on the street. The number of Adamant guards also increased uncomfortably. Right on time, a panel of three Adamants, NCOs by my guess, pounded their paws on the podium and called the proceedings to order. There were many LGMs milling about, along with a handful of locals. The LGMs were staring blankly at the items to be auctioned. The locals stared intently at the ground.

"The first item for auction is this hay binder. It works well. Let the bidding start at five percent of crop quota for two months," said the dog in the middle.

A green mitt went up.

"I have five for two."

An LGM said quietly, "Five for three."

"Do I hear five for four?" I didn't see anyone flinch, but he said, "I have five for four."

"Six for four," said a local.

"Your bid is rejected. We took this binder from you because you were short on your last two quotas," said the central Adamant.

"But without it, I'll be short again," the fellow whined.

"If so, you will be executed. Do I hear five for five?" He

waited only a second to slap the countertop. "Sold. The next item is..."

I inched toward the farmer whose bid was rejected. When I arrived, he stood right where he'd been, shoulders drooping, mouth agape. He was in a world of hurt.

"Sorry to hear of your troubles, citizen," I whispered.

Suddenly realizing it was I who spoke and it was to him, he turned to look at me. "I failed to make quota and paid with my machine. The Adamant were right to take it."

Ah, he figured I was trying to get him to express resentment.

"And if they kill you next month, you'll sing the same tune?"

He furrowed his brow. "I have no idea what you're talking about," he replied, and he stormed away.

Okay, cross making friends with Mr. Sour Puss off my to-do list.

The next few pieces went quickly to LGMs for what seemed like bargains. Then again, what did I know? The final item was the largest. It was a solar-powered electronic harvester. It resembled a child's toy to me, but it was probably a big deal here.

"The bidding will start at ten percent for six months," said the barker. That was a pretty high price.

It took a moment, but finally an LGM raised a digit.

"Ten for seven?"

"A week of slave labor," said a woman behind me.

"The current bid would be *three* weeks of slave labor," responded the Adamant without emotion.

"Three weeks," shot back the woman.

"Do I hear four weeks or ten for seven?"

An LGM said, "ten for seven."

The woman slumped.

The Adamant looked to her. "Do you bid four weeks?"

She began slowly shaking her head. At barely a whisper she said, "I can't pay that much."

To my great surprise, out of my mouth popped, "Two weeks for myself and two for my wife." I pointed to the woman as I backed up quickly to stand by her.

"Do I hear more?" Again, in an instant he slapped his paw. "Sold. The winners will please report to me and provide their names. Sentences will commence at dawn tomorrow."

The woman stared at me with burning fury. I think she wanted to bore right through my fool head with her eyes. She locked her elbow in mine with a jerk and pulled me forward. In a voice meant only for me, she hissed, "You're going to get us both *killed*."

"No..." I started to respond, but she stomped down on my foot to silence me.

I contemplated saying *ouch*, but decided she might have a point about us being in mortal danger, so I canned it.

We stood in front of the Adamant until he decided we'd waited long enough. "Names."

"Cellardoor Pontared and husband," she said through clinched teeth.

"Husband is not an acceptable name," he snapped back.

"Josbelub's his name. Josbelub Pontared," she said casually.

"Does he speak?" snarled the Adamant.

"Of course, I do. I'm Josbelub, just like the lady said."

He tapped a screen. "We show the Cellardoor, but not the Josbelub. Please clarify." He looked right at me. His paw slipped to the top of his side arm.

"My man was away at the time of the census and returned but two days ago. He hasn't had time to register yet," she said quickly.

"That was quite some time ago. Where could he...," he focused on me instead, "where were you all that time?"

I replied quickly, "I was at sea."

Simultaneously, Cellardoor piped in, "He was away trading."

The dog's hand fondled his pistol grip.

"I was away at sea *trading*. I went to Harmark. The return voyage was one big storm blowing in the wrong direction. I nearly sank more times than I barfed."

One of the other Adamant snickered at my response.

"Silence, Wedgelet, or you'll serve by their side."

That wiped the mirth off his muzzle.

"Very well. Register today, and both of you report to the sewage plant at dawn tomorrow. Any questions?"

"No, sir," she responded for us both. With that she tugged me away as fast as decorum would allow. My new wife sure was a bundle of nerves.

SIX

Finally, they were roughly pulled from their seats and walked a long way into some structure. Mirri couldn't tell if it was a ship or a ground-based building. After being tossed into metal chairs, they were left alone, or at least in silence, for nearly an hour. A door opened, a chair squeaked, and their restraints were removed.

There sat Malraff behind a desk, scribbling with an old-fashioned pen on paper. She acted like she was unaware the teens were there.

After a few minutes, she set her pen down and leaned back in her chair, stretching and smiling.

"Ah, there. Now I've finished all the official nonsense. Now for the fun portion of the project." She folded her paws and looked to the teens. "I'm certain you have a million questions. I'll answer none of them. The project you're involved in and the acts of participation required of you will be made clear at the time they arise. Fortunately, foreknowledge is *not* required for your full and complete participation."

Mirri sat up straight. "You saw how close Jon Ryan came to saving us and killing you. I warned you before that if you harm us you'll regret it. I will repeat that warning one more time. Release us or die."

Malraff bobbed her head as if seriously considering Mirri's threat.

"Let-me-think-about-it-no," she slurred into one sentence. Then she giggled at her witty response. "My dear foolish child. Uncle Jon came as close as he ever will to freeing you or laying a finger on me. His luck was better than he could have prayed for. In addition, he will never find us. If he can't locate the three of us, he cannot make the world right, now can he?"

"How could he have found us before?"

"While that might normally be an excellent point, it is not relevant here. Yes, it was stunning that he located you. But he cannot repeat that magic. We are in a place he cannot know of and could not breech, were he to find its location by divine intervention."

"You've been warned," Mirri said harshly.

"Well thank you for that courtesy, child. I'll make you a promise. If he finds us and stands in front of us before you are dead and gone, I will put this gun," she patted her side arm, "to this part of my head," she tapped her temple, "and blow my own brains out."

"As that will likely be a chaotic moment, maybe you'd like to practice once or twice right now," Mirri braved.

"Enough sarcasm and disrespect. Tomorrow, the idiot physician the idiot emperor assigned will arrive to meddle and get underfoot. At that point, we will settle in with a vengeance to find out what we wish to know. Until then, I invite you to rest, relax, and refresh as my honored guests." She jerked her head to one side while glaring at a guard.

The kids were lifted from their seats and carried down a

short hall. Two adjacent metal doors slid open, and one teen was thrown into each room. Then the doors snapped shut with a resounding clang. Mirri quickly took stock of the room. It was harsh and sparse. A bed without a mattress and a hole in the floor. There was a water spigot directly above the hole. That was it. Ah, she thought, how the mighty have fallen. From the lap of luxury to the pit of despair all in one day. She was left alone the remainder of the day. They served a correspondingly sparse meal several hours later, but at least she was otherwise undisturbed.

Mirraya awoke to two surprises. One was that she had fallen asleep on the impossible bed. The other was that Sentorip was rousing her.

"Wake, Mastress," she said softly. "The high seer calls for you."

Mirri sat up and rubbed her face, taking a moment to orient herself. "What, no bath?"

Sentorip smiled faintly. "No. The high seer is less fussy than His Imperial Lord."

"Plus, with the mess she plans to make of me, why bother, right?"

Sentorip got a profoundly concerned look on her face. "Don't even joke about such things. The high seer is stern and direct, which is to say she's Adamant. But she would never be cruel."

"You don't know what's going on, do you?" Then it hit Mirri that they were almost certainly being monitored. She patted Sentorip's shoulder. "I'm sorry. You're probably right. I wake up grumpy sometimes, that's all."

Sentorip smiled back.

"So, I'm most pleasantly surprised to see you here," said Mirraya.

"The high seer does not have Descore here, even for

herself." There was clear judgment in her tone. Who didn't need servants? "His Imperial Lord himself suggested Darfey and I come along to ease the seer's burden."

Hmm. Malraff would be pissed at that. She couldn't very well turn down an imperial offer, but if she wanted niceties, she'd have arranged for them herself. Mirraya worried for the Descore's safety. They would never suspect how much they were resented by one very powerful, very mean Adamant bitch.

"You are well?" Sentorip asked as she smoothed out the garments Mirri wore. No change of clothes was offered, so she was determined to have her mastress look as good as the situation allowed.

"Yes, thanks for asking. And you two?"

Sentorip furrowed her brow. No one had ever asked her that before. "Yes, we are," she replied mechanically. Back to her usual tone, she said, "Come. It will anger the high seer if you keep her waiting." She gestured toward the hole and turned her back to Mirri.

They emerged into the corridor just as Slapgren and Darfey did also. A trio of guards awaited them. A grunt directed the Deft to move. The Descore remained behind without having to be asked. The teens walked a short distance to an unassuming door, and a second grunt indicated they should halt. One soldier knocked softly on the door, and it glided open.

"You may remain in the corridor," called out Malraff. "Send the specimens in."

Slapgren whispered to Mirraya, "That doesn't sound too promising."

Her eyes silently agreed with his observation.

Malraff was leaning back on her desk, facing the teens as they entered. "School begins in earnest today, kiddies."

Neither responded.

"Good, no back talk. Maybe this will be more pleasant than I anticipated."

For *you* maybe, thought Mirri. She'd learned better than to give voice to her feelings.

"Today you will each be tested. Various samples will be collected. Blood, semen, tissue biopsies, that sort of thing."

Slapgren glanced to Mirraya in horror, having clearly heard the word semen. He knew who'd be giving *that* sample. It was the how of it that concerned him deeply.

"The idiot physician Pastersal will cling to me and be under paw the entire time. Hopefully I won't have to kill him this early on, but I'm not in the mood for nonsense. We'll have to see."

Malraff looked intently at them. "If you two pests behave yourselves and cooperate, today won't be too bad." Her lips curled to a snarly smile. "Tomorrow, not so much."

The door opened and a male Adamant entered. That he hadn't asked permission clearly irritated Malraff. His fatal accident would now happen much sooner than later.

"Ah, High Seer," he said, studying a handheld he was carrying, "I'm glad you're here. We may begin immediately."

Malraff's tense physical response predicted Pastersal's longevity, or lack thereof. She didn't respond other than to point the Deft toward a pair of exam tables. That they could easily double as torture tables too was not lost on either teen.

Needles of an impressive number and size range appeared. The teens were bombarded with pokes, prods, and other sharp impositions. Then Malraff handed Slapgren a plastic cup. "Semen sample," was all she said.

"Wh...what, here...now?" he responded incredulously.

"Yes, here and now. Otherwise I'll cut off your testicle to get the sample. Please don't be modest."

"But how'm I supposed to —"

"Point and shoot," said Malraff. She then stared at Slapgren's groin in anticipation of the sample-gathering procedure.

Fortunately, Slapgren, being in his teenage bloom, could generate a good sample quickly enough. He almost lost his ability after Mirraya, sensing his humiliation, offered to help. That had nearly incapacitated him completely.

Malraff snatched the cup from Slapgren without a word and handed it off to an assistant.

"We require a brain biopsy now," said Pastersal as casually as he might order a sandwich at a deli.

"What?" snapped Mirraya.

"Don't worry. After we take the biopsies, we'll suspend the stasis field long enough for you two to heal," responded Pastersal.

"Assuming, of course, the biopsies don't cause so much damage you can't think straight to transform," added Malraff maliciously.

"Now, High Seer, I don't see any reason to frighten our specimens more than necessary," chided Pastersal.

Mirri reflected that Pastersal was such a humanitarian, so kind and visionary for an Adamant.

True to their word, after the highly invasive core samples removed from the teens' brains, they were allowed to heal while they still could. Then the stasis field was turned back on and the teens were escorted back to their cells.

Mirraya was relieved to see Sentorip awaiting her, a tray of food in her arms, sitting on a newly arrived mattress.

"So, it wasn't so bad, was it?" asked Sentorip.

"Nah, piece of cake. See," Mirraya pointed to herself generally, "not a mark on me."

SEVEN

As Cellardoor—by the way, I definitely had to press her on the origins of her name—and I walked toward her house, I started to speak a couple times, but she shut me down. Once it was an elbow to the ribs, another time a look that hurt even more. I was certain she was angry with me. Touchy people, these Uglaies.

When we arrived, she opened the door and shoved me in. The door shut heavily behind us.

"Well, you've got all the nerve," she said. "Pulling a stunt like that will get us both killed." She glared at me. "You, a'course, I couldn't care less about. Good riddance, I'd say. But me? I have three hungry little ones to feed and protect. Where'd they be without their ma? Hmm, you lame brain. Did you think a'that?"

I tried to look sheepish but darn cute.

"Clearly you didn't. Now we're between them. We lied to the Adamant and we need to hide you from the town folk. Damn you, I say. We'll never pull either off. Then we'll be dead *and* humiliated."

"Which is worse? I mean, we could try and angle the damage such that..."

"*Enough*. It's far bad enough you endanger me. I'll not abide a twisted wit to boot."

"I'm Jon, by the way, but you can still call me Josbelub if you'd prefer."

"I don't care who you are. You're a curse, that's all I know. What the devils got into you back there? Why'd you up my bid and include yourself?"

"Because you looked like you needed help—a friend."

"If I were to need a friend, I'd not come shopping in your store. As to needing help, who doesn't? But that stunt'll like as much get us killed. If the Adamant don't figure it out, a neighbor will surely try to get in their good graces by selling me out."

"Am I to assume there's no Mr. Pontared at this particular moment? That would complicate things a bit."

"No, thank the Six Heavens. He's dead nearly a year. The Adamant took a dislike to him, and that was all there was to him."

"Sorry to hear that. I truly am."

"Well I'm not. He was a drunkard and a thief. Either quality will bring the Adamant down on a body. Both are positively lethal."

"What do you want that harvester for? You know, *our* new harvester."

"I wanted it to chop carrots with. What do you think I wanted it for? It's to harvest *crops*."

"I didn't see any out back."

"I mean to rent it out, make a steady profit."

"Well, you have my blessing."

"I didn't ask for your blessing, nor do I require it. Plus, being dead makes running a business out of the question."

"Don't be so negative. I'm sure we'll pull this off. What can go wrong?"

"Oh, I don't know. Let me see. One, you're an alien. No local'd marry one. Two, you forced me to lie to the Adamant. Three, my neighbors are a snoopy gossipy lot. There's no hiding a juicy bit like this."

"Tell them we are married, that true love forced us together."

"Are you daft? I just said no one'd marry an alien. It's unholy, unnatural."

"What about true love?"

"We're done talking about it. We'll meet at the sewage plant each day, but otherwise you avoid this place like the plague house."

"We don't have a perfect marriage, do we? Say, where are my stepchildren? I love kids."

"They're in school, and you'll never see them."

"Look, all kidding aside, I have money. Can't we pay off our debt and be done with it?"

"No. That's ridiculous. The Adamant don't take payment. They want productivity."

"How about a bribe?"

"Now I know you're daft *and* an alien. Adamant don't take bribes."

"I'm sure this will work out just fine. Look, I'll do the whole month. You take care of your kids and no one will be the wiser."

"You can't do my two weeks. A deal with the Adamant is a deal. End of story."

"What do they care who does the work?"

"No means no. Drop it."

"I passed a sewage plant earlier today. Are we working at

the one near that tall tower, the one with the plants growing up the sides?"

"Yes, that's the one."

"I'll be there at first light."

With that, I left. She wasn't warming to me like I'd planned. I needed to interact with the locals and the Adamant to try and see if I could discover a weakness. Cellardoor was closed to me. Hopefully that would change. Huh. Cellardoor was closed. I was a pretty funny robot.

I made it to the plant just at first light. Cellardoor was already there. She had a knapsack that I presumed held her lunch. I didn't wonder hard whether she'd packed for two. A detail of Adamant arrived maybe half an hour later. Apparently, they never traveled alone. A low-ranking officer came over to us and said, "You will be working in the clean-out chutes today. The shovels are over there, and the picks are over there if you need them. Be warned. If any of us think either of you are working at too casual a pace, neither of you will receive credit for today, and one additional day will be added to your commitment."

"Don't worry about me," I replied cheerily. "Hard work is my middle name."

"You are Josbelub Pontared. That is the only identification we require. Your middle name is not necessary."

"No, I meant I work so hard that *could* be my middle name."

"We still do not require a third name. Are you stalling? Stalling is unacceptable."

"No. I'm getting to work." I was tempted to ask when lunch was because I hated to be bossed around, but I let it go. Cellardoor already held a shovel, and I didn't want her to use it on me.

What could I say about cleaning sewage lines that isn't

self-evident? It turned out to be a sweltering day. There was no breeze, and the only chill in the air came off Cellardoor in my direction. The smell was horrific, the slimy ooze was gross, and even with all my sensors turned off, I still couldn't avoid the stench. Oh, and I slipped and face-planted in the goo—twice. Hell, those were the only smiles I drew from my wife all day.

For her part, Cellardoor worked hard at a steady clip. I was impressed. I could only imagine what the sensory overload must have been like by late afternoon. But she kept her head down and forged ahead. We were given thirty minutes for lunch, which was our only break. Pitchers of water were available nearby, and I made it a point to drink often.

As we made for the shade during lunch, Cellardoor said, "Wash up and I'll spread the meal over there." She nodded toward a spot under a few large trees. Bless her heart, she did pack for two. "Be quick about it. They'll be calling us back promptly on time."

"Yes, ma'am," I said with a half-salute. That got a tiny grin from her. Maybe she was coming around to the charm of Jon Ryan. How could she not?

"It's not much, but it's all I can spare," she remarked as she set out cheese, bread, and dried fruits. "Between the kids and the Adamant, there's not much food left for me."

"Us, you mean," I said with a charming wink.

"I meant me. I couldn't risk not bringing my husband his lunch, too. If the Adamant noticed, they'd get suspicious. Everything makes them suspicious."

"Tell me about it," I replied as I bit off a chunk of bread.

"It's good to know you have a lick of sense then. Be mindful of them at all times. I still don't know why they haven't wiped us out like I hear tell they do most other worlds."

"I think we're too small to devote many resources to. If that's the case, they need us around for now to keep production up," I remarked as I swatted away a couple of the many annoying cats roaming feral. These two had designs on my cheese.

"What do you mean *we*? Any fool can see you're not one of us."

"Those fools can't." I pointed some cheese at the Adamant where they lounged, eating their lunch, too.

"I noticed. Odd. They seem to be so thorough otherwise."

"They don't see what they're not looking for," I mumbled as I chewed a tough piece of fruit. It was sour and bitter. Yuck. "What is this?" I asked, holding the piece up.

She guffawed through her nose. "That's the healing wax, you bumpkin. Give it here. I brought it in case either of us got hurt."

"Well, at least my throat is safe for the while."

"You are an odd one, Josbelub Pontared, I have to tell you that." She held up the lump of wax. "As it's also a powerful laxative, your innards will be healthy in no time at all, too."

We both chuckled at that.

"Five minutes," shouted the officer. "If you have to lift a leg, do it now."

"It seems counterproductive to pee when you're cleaning the very sewer you'd be using," I remarked.

"Aye," she replied. "That's why I think I'll try that bush over there." She pointed to a shrub as she stood and stretched.

"I'll wait until you're out of sight and lift my leg against this tree, if it's okay with the missus."

"If you see her, you can ask her," Cellardoor said over a shoulder.

As she walked away, I swear she swayed her hips more than she did before.

The next two days were wash-rinse-repeat. We cleaned those chutes but good. We stank to high heaven, and we became co-conspirators, if not friends. Cellardoor was a reserved individual. Maybe she was that way by nature, or maybe life and the war had made her so. What little more she told me about her dead husband made me cringe. He was one filthy heel.

Dawn of day four brought trouble. Slave labor with a pretend wife couldn't be too easy.

"Today we are sending you to the solid waste disposal station in Ainsbury to repair storm damage," said a high-ranking officer we hadn't seen previously.

"Ainsbury?" said Cellardoor. "That's quite a long way. We won't get much done in one day."

The Adamant officer, whose name turned out to be Group-Single Fuffefer—may his soul be tormented in hell forever—visibly ground his teeth before responding. "Slaves will not question assignments. You will be there until I decide the task is complete. It may take several days. Now get aboard the truck."

"Several days? What about my...our children? We haven't made plans for their care. If you'll allow one of us..."

"*Silence.*" Fuffefer was hot. "Slaves and their children have no rights. You will mount the truck, or you will be shot. What becomes of your demon spawn is no concern of mine." The dog was serious. I believe xenophobic best described him.

I noticed a withered old woman was slowly approaching. She was crooked, her cane was crooked, and her path was crooked. I made a hasty plan and set it in motion before the light of reason could dissuade me.

In my head, I said, *one fiber, along the ground, to the soldier nearest on the left.*

A solitary fiber shot from my left index finger and snaked over to the guard.

Sleep, I said. That generally worked. I really hoped it did presently.

The Adamant lay down where he stood, cuddling his rifle like it was a fluffy teddy bear. Perfect.

"Ah, excuse me, your highness," I said. "Is he coming, too?" I fingered the snoozing guard. "If so, I'll try and wake him if you want."

That stunt had a better effect on Fuffefer than I could have hoped for. After shaking like a tree in a mighty wind, he unholstered his side arm.

"You lazy, incompetent slacker," he howled.

Then he began firing at the ground around the guard. That woke him right up. The stunned soldier popped to his feet like a jack-in-the-box and, bless his heart, saluted Fuffefer as he tried to stop trembling.

"What in the name of all service makes you think..."

I stopped listening to Fuffefer's dressing down of the guard. The old woman had finally gotten as close to us as she was going to, about two meters away. I sidestepped over to her, keeping an eye on the Adamant. The two other soldiers had their eyes riveted on their unfortunate comrade.

"Ma'am, a saintly favor. Do you know Cellardoor?" I pointed to my coworker.

The woman strained forward and studied her. "Ah, yes, the drunkard's wife. That man..."

"He died. Look, here's some money. Look after her kids a few days. The Adamant are taking us away." I stuffed what cash I had into her gnarled hand.

"The Adamant are taking you to play?" She placed the money directly under her nose and angled what must have been her better eye at it. "Why pay me to play with..."

"Away," I said too loud. One of the guards heard and spun toward me.

"Protect Cellardoor's children," I shouted as I closed her fingers around the coins. I took one step back and raised my arms at the crone. "No, stop. The Group-Single has the situation in hand."

The guard who'd noticed came up and shoved his gun in my ribs. "What's going on here? You were trying to escape."

"No. This worthy citizen noticed the commotion and came to help the Group-Single if help was needed. I was reassuring her no aid was required. That's all."

He eyed her dubiously. "You were coming to our aid?" he huffed.

"No, I said I won't *play*. What are you two lunatics going on about? I'm an old woman and I'm babysitting that woman's children. I don't have time for such nonsense." With that, she turned and slowly staggered away. She tossed a disgusted hand back at us as she departed.

"She meant well. Silly old woman," I said to the still scowling Adamant

The guard was about to respond, but he spun when Fuffefer set off a long volley at the soldier I'd put to sleep. This time Fuffefer aimed at the guy's head. By the time the guard and I turned, that head was only a red-pink vapor puff.

"Now everyone get *aboard* that *train* or I'll shoot you *all*." Fuffefer sounded convincing.

Everyone double-timed it onto the train and it lurched into movement.

Cellardoor stared at me aghast.

"What?" I said. "I didn't do anything." I gestured over my shoulder. "That guard decided to take a nap at the wrong time, that's all." Then, because I had to, I winked at her.

EIGHT

The garbage dump cleanup, which is really an oxymoronic process, lasted five days. It went well for a few reasons. First, Cellardoor was impressed with how I'd rushed to the aid of her kids. Second, we were cleaning rubbish, not sewers. It was a real step up in the world. Third, possibly because he was still embarrassed about how his guard fell asleep, Fuffefer lightened up on us quite a bit. Don't get me wrong, he was still a certified grade-AA jerk, but the hateful edge seemed to be missing. Those five days turned out to be the most pleasant slave labor stint I'd ever pulled.

Fuffefer arranged for a truck to bring our group back to Fottot. He dropped Cellardoor and me off at our marital residence around dusk. Again, that seemed like a nicer gesture than he should have performed.

As I hopped down from the truck bed, Fuffefer came around to speak to me. "You are a hard worker, Josbelub Pontared. On missions such as these, I mostly deal with people trying to do as little as possible. Never once did you attempt that. In fact, you worked with a dedication I would never have expected from someone in your position."

Uh-oh. Was this leading somewhere where I ended up dead?

"You would have no way of knowing, being a farmer or whatever it is you said you did, but these assignments are not my favorite. I'm a warrior. I would serve the empire in battle, not puppysitting. Anyway, you made it not loathsome for me, so thank you."

"I'll try and keep it up the next five days," I responded.

"Very well," he replied stiffly. "Tomorrow, you will be separated. You will work clearing debris around buildings. Your bitch will report to the construction site at the main square. She'll cook for the crews. I'll send this truck for you both at dawn."

All right then. I'd be spending the night with the missus. We'd have to keep up appearances, right? Wouldn't Cellardoor be pleased?

As the truck drove away, she and I stood at the side of the street. "Good riddance," she hissed when they were gone.

"Aw, I think they're warming up to us. Fuffefer's even sending the truck to pick us up tomorrow at dawn."

It took only milliseconds for her to process the implications of my remark. "He said no such thing."

"It'd be a shame to disappoint him, me not being here bright and early. I think you'll be pretty unhappy when you find out that's what he said and have to explain where the love of your existence was." I wagged my eyebrows.

"Just when I'm deluding myself into thinking you're not all that bad, you drop to a new level of being an ass."

"You're not going to believe this, but you're not the first woman to tell me that."

"I not only believe it, I know it for a certainty." She

stomped a foot on the pavement. "Well, let's get inside. The longer the neighbors are gawking at us, the worse this'll turn out."

I extended an elbow. "May I escort the lady of the house?"

"You may not live to see tomorrow if you keep it up," she said as she stormed away. Lots of spirit, that wife of mine.

Even as I entered, three darling-looking kids in the range of four to eight were group-hugging mom's waist. The old woman who'd watched them clumped into the room, leaning heavily on her cane. She looked exhausted.

"Ah, Mrs. Weldsot, I can't thank you enough..." Cellardoor began to say.

Weldsot jerked a hang-on-a-minute hand. "I'm too tired to be listening to anything. I'll bid you both a g'night and be on my way." She angled toward the door.

"Surely you'll spend one more night. It's late and you live..."

"Close enough. No, I'll lay my head on my own pillow tonight. And don't ye bother offering to walk me home, Mr. Pontared. I'll not be seen with a drunkard at any hour, especially a late one such as this."

By the time Cellardoor was finished, Weldsot was already out the door and gone.

"I guess she thinks I'm your dead husband."

"Or that I only wed drunks. She has a vicious tongue, that woman. But, seeing how I owe her so much, I'll not mention that."

"Ah, I think you already did."

She looked me up and down. "Yeah, but you are a drunkard. You'll never remember." She really couldn't help herself. She smiled and began to chuckle. "All right. Let's get the lot of you to bed," she announced loudly as she herded the kids toward the back of the house.

I raised a hand. "Am I in the lot?"

"You most certainly are not. You're on the couch, and I'm pleased to say it's lumpier than it looks. Good night, sir."

The family disappeared down a hallway, but I could hear their chatter until the last of them was asleep half an hour later. I sat on the couch thinking back on my families, my kids too excited to sleep. I missed them. I missed them all. I missed Mirri and Slapgren, too, maybe even a bit more.

The next few days of labor were a breeze. I was certain Fuffefer was giving us cushy assignments. Maybe there weren't any horrible jobs currently available. Either way, Cellardoor didn't mind cooking for a bunch of hardworking men. I certainly didn't mind cleaning up Fuffefer's backyard. Yeah, that was the "debris around building" back-breaker he'd mentioned. Hey, I didn't miss the sewer or the dump. By the time our two-week sentence was up, old Fuffefer's yard was the envy of the entire neighborhood.

He came out to watch me finish that last afternoon. "I mentioned you were a hard worker, Josbelub Pontared."

"Yes, you did. Thank you."

"It is not a compliment, it is merely an observation." He rested his arms behind his back and rocked on his hind legs. "Your people are strange to me, Josbelub Pontared. Many conquered races are, I suppose. But yours is most peculiar to me."

Hmm. Where oh where was this heading?

"How so?"

"They seem lifeless and empty."

That was a strange opinion. "Could you be more specific? I don't see us like that."

"Oh, you wouldn't. You're too close to them, naturally."

"Naturally," I agreed.

I flashed on an image of Cellardoor's face, one where we

were close together. She didn't look lifeless and empty to me. There was a strength and calm in her eyes. No, not strength, *certainty*. Yes. She was calm and certain and, that was it, she was contented. I rifled through files of as many locals as I could quickly. Yup. They all had the same tranquil bliss on their faces. Odd I hadn't articulated it until then. Here these people are conquered by the nastiest of invaders, and they're still happy.

"The look that bothers you is one of contentment, I think. They are a fundamentally happy race. It's all a matter of focusing on the good and trying to downplay the bad."

"You said *they*."

Oops. I needed to be more careful.

"That is a telling slip of the tongue, Josbelub Pontared, because you are the only one of them who is missing that look. In your eyes I see longing, I see pain, and mostly I see fight. You are unique among your people in that *you* are a warrior." He grunted a laugh. "I'm sorry I didn't confront you as we swept across this fart-bubble of a planet." He closed his eyes and smiled. "That would have been a worthy battle, you and me."

He opened his eyes and looked down. "Oh, your people *resisted* us, but they had no heart for the fight, for the killing. They had lost the war before our first ship landed. Pitiful wretches."

This Fuffefer was smarter than he looked. I just prayed he didn't intuit any more about me.

"Don't the Adamant experience contentment, moments of peace?"

He looked at me critically. He was uncomfortable divulging either personal or potentially strategic insights. Then his face eased. He was, I think he realized, talking to a slave who'd be dead sooner than he could have imagined.

"No. Those are alien emotions, literally. They have no utility. They can in no way advance the empire."

"What if there comes a time that the empire no longer needs to expand? You'd be better off having such releases before you hit the wall emotionally."

He squinted. "You are a worldly male. That is a well-constructed and logical observation. Again, you are unique among your otherwise dull, unmotivated species. That time will never come. The empire has expanded for longer than our records can reveal. Much longer than anyone can remember, to be certain. Why, warrior among sheep, would we stop conquering?"

"When you control enough. It happens to all races. They rise, they dominate, then, surely, they ebb. Their time passes, and they return to the cosmic dust."

He harrumphed.

"Have you ever seen or heard of a human, a former inhabitant of Earth?"

"No," he shot back. "Why?"

"They once controlled a significant part of this galaxy. They spread among the cosmos and were as numerous as the stars in the sky. Now, you've never even heard of them. If the Adamant meet a similar fate, having cultivated a set of softer emotions would be handy. Just sayin'."

"And how is it you do know of them, Ungalaymian farmer?"

"Do you recall that big building on the main square, the one with the statues in front of it?"

"Yes, of course."

"And do you recall what happened to it?"

"Certainly. We blew it to pieces."

"That was our main library. It contained books and data

files older than the dust we are standing on. That's how I know of that lost civilization."

"Ah. Well, such knowledge is not productive. It's good we resolved the issue. No one will miss the library."

"I do."

He shuffled his paws in the dust. "It might have kept you from the hard work that you do so well."

"And I'd be either more content and happy or more lifeless and empty, depending on who you ask."

"Things will be changing on this planet soon, Josbelub Pontared. I can tell you no more, but change is coming. I would offer you a chance to serve me as my assistant. You would be less subject to...the changes."

Sounded like the time for accommodating the locals was nearing an end. The LGM must be about to take on all the grunt work.

"And my family? Does that umbrella cover them too?"

"Why worry about your family? Would you allow concerns for them to hold you back?"

"Are you serious?"

"I am always serious. Why would you?"

"Because they're my family. I love them."

He shook his head in an irritated manner. "You see, again, this sentimentality is so counterproductive. Among my kind, family is who spawned you. Our allegiance, *my* sole allegiance, is to the pack. To the empire."

"To each his own, for now." I couldn't help that last jab, unwise as it was.

"If you serve me as a house servant, I will allow your family to come also. But you must promise I will never see or hear from your pups." He held up a claw. "Not once. Is that acceptable?"

"It is. When do I start?"

"You already have." He swept an arm across his backyard. "My Packlet-Wedge will show you to your quarters. Then you may retrieve your precious family." With that, he spun on a heel and walked into his house.

Oh boy. Cellardoor was not going to take the news of her new home well. But, hey, I was her husband. She had to obey me, right?

NINE

She finished counting to eight in her head to calm herself. "No, I have not. I have many duties. The experimentation on the—"

"Whatever it is you do can't be more important than this. I'm afraid I'll have to insist you make the study of the Deft your number-one priority." He squinted his muzzle to hike his glasses up as he glared at her.

When she'd finished counting to sixteen, she folded her paws gently in front of her. They happened to be right next to the blaster, by chance. "I will consider your opinion, Physician Level *Six* Pastersal." She really hit the *six* hard, to make certain he recalled it was less than Level Twelve. That would still have been below her rank, but only just.

He absently glanced at the insignia on his sleeve, then set the reams of paper on her desk. "This is part of the results. These are generally histological and gross anatomical data. There's some physiology, but most of those tests are still pending."

"Why don't you set them on my desk," she said after he had.

"I just did," he said, confused.

"Then I thank you. You see, if you had set something on my desk without asking permission first," she picked up the gun, "I'd be forced to kill you." She aimed right between his eyes. Her paw was as steady as a rock.

Pastersal licked nervously at his lips. Finally, he said, "I'm not sure that's an appropriate jest, Malraff."

"You are correct. It is not a jest." She moved her hand a fraction to one side and whizzed a bolt so close to his ear it drew blood.

He squealed like the frightened dog he was and jumped backward. "Don't think that I won't report this outrage to His Imperial Lord personally."

"Oh, I think you won't." She sliced a matching nick in his other ear. "If you did, I might become so distracted that my aim would fail me. Trust me, you couldn't live with yourself if that were the case." She set the gun down gently and smiled up at him. "Now, were you just about to say you would take these documents with you and be in your laboratory studying them like a first-year student?"

"Y...yes."

"And that with all your duties, I'm not likely to see you for at least three days, and only then if I were to send for you?"

"Y...yes," he growled back.

"Good day and good luck to you then. Leave the door as you found it—*closed*." She pivoted her chair and, with her back to him, opened a document on a large screen.

TEN

"So, you cut a deal to move my children—who are not *your* children, lest you've forgotten—and me into that monster's house so we can be his permanent slaves? And you did all that without bothering to ask me first?"

"You could summarize it that way *if* you were being tragically unfair to me," I sheepishly responded.

"Well that *is* how I see it, and the answer is no, ten *thousand* times no. I'd rather die than lick his paws."

"That, my love, may be the actual choice you're making. The one for your kids *too*, I hate to add."

"One, don't ever call me *love*." She raised a threatening digit. "*Ever*. Two, why are you always so *damn* dramatic?"

"My burning ears. You're swearing? Now I know the universe is about to come crashing to an end."

"You...you bring it out of a body, even one that abhors such language." She wagged a finger at me this time.

In spite of the tension in the air, something hit me. The way she did the finger thing. It was so human. I thought back to all the digits and digit-like appendages I'd seen in my long

55

life. Yes. Her finger was distinct and different in a very human manner. I took a long, hard scientific look at her. There was human in her. In all the Uglaies. Was I talking to my distant relative?

"Cellardoor, I'm going to do something important you probably won't like. There's no risk or harm, so bear with me."

I raised my left hand at her.

"I was married to a lousy man. I know what comes next, and I *forbid* it."

"It's not what you think."

"Ya. That's what he always—"

I cut her off by shooting my probe fibers. They gently enveloped her. They also rapidly shut her up. She froze, except for her eyes, which bounded in every direction trying to take in what was happening.

In my head, I asked, *What are you? Genetics and physiology.*

Female, age thirty-three years Earth standard. G4:P3, currently cycling in menses. Organs are all typical of Homo sapiens, though spleen is much smaller. Brain volume consistent with human values. DNA has twenty-three paired helical strands. Homology with Homo sapiens' DNA display eighteen percent divergence. Approximately twenty-three thousand coding genes ...

I stopped the report. She was as human as I was. Two billion years of evolution had altered her. The inhabitants of Ungalaym were like those of the Galapagos back when there was such an island chain. Isolated from their main gene pool, they drifted to become a new species. But they retained much of their original nature. Her DNA was tweaked, but it was a certainty where it had evolved from. I had been looking for the humans in this timeline. I had just forgot to recall Professor Darwin's laws. They were right in front of me. We *had* survived. All my efforts, all my suffering wasn't for naught.

Well frack me with a laser beam set on high, I had done good. I was talking with one of my N^{th} removed grandkids.

Then I snapped back to the reality of Cellardoor's tongue-lashing.

"What in the name of the three heavens was that, and how dare you do that to me with or without my permission? And what's that glazed, stupefied, lobotomized look in your eyes? Hmm? Cat got your tongue?"

Crap, at the dump, there were cats all over the place. We'd brought kitty cats with us into the far future. Dang, I bet there were rats too. Always with the rats. We tried to keep them contained, but I bet they lurked in the walls of Cellardoor's house and nibbled at her cheese.

The resounding slap on my face returned me to present times.

"What'd you do that for?" I asked, rubbing my cheek instinctively.

"If you have to *ask,* you wouldn't understand the answer. *Out.* I want you out of my home, out of my life, and most of all out of the reach of whatever devil's-own handiwork you just violated me with."

"Tell me of your people, Cellardoor. Where did they come from? What is your origin myth?"

She did not expect those questions. She sat back down and seemed to visually scan the floor for a response.

"I'm sorry I did what I did. I am a lot different than you can imagine. I had to."

"I'm beginning to believe you are more than a lot different." The stunned look vanished. "Who and what are you, Jon Ryan? Are you an angel? A demon from perdition sent to test me?"

57

I chuckled softly. "Neither such extreme, my dear. You want the long or the short version?"

"I want the *truth*," she replied, setting her jaw.

Oh boy. This was going to take a while.

Three hours, eight intrusions by kids, two potty breaks for her, and five cups of tea later, I'd pretty much brought Cellardoor up to speed on my wild story. After the first fifteen minutes she even stopped bothering to interrupt me and listened with her mouth agape.

"That's a truly unbelievable story, Jon."

"Yet here I sit before you. Plus, I do wish to remind you of the need to respect your elders."

"There you go. You create this magical moment, and then you bash it by being an ass."

"Yeah. Aren't I wonderful?"

"That is not the word that's flashing in my mind." She sipped her cold tea. "I've so many questions, I don't know where to begin."

"There's no rush. The only rush is to get your family to the relative safety of Fuffefer's household."

"But why? You could fly us away in your spaceship. If the Adamant are going to rain holy hell down on us again, why risk hanging around for the final moment?"

"No can do. I'm here on a mission. I need to infiltrate the Adamant and save my kids, like I said. If I leave now I'll be bailing on a good opportunity. It's really better than I could have prayed for."

"But, you could save *some* of us. We're your *kin*, Jon Ryan. Maybe your mission needs to change?"

Oh crap. Now came the tough part, the part she couldn't possibly understand or accept.

"No, Cellardoor. That's not how it's going down. Before you ask why or try to sway me, let me tell you why." I took a deep breath. "In my two billion years of experience, I've come to know a few things as absolutes. One is that evil will always come looking for you, and it will always find you. It'll generally win, too. Even if you somehow come out on top, the losses are staggering. I mean that internally, to your soul. People are going to die at the hands of evil. They always have and always will. I can't change that. Believe me, I've tried. It can't be done.

"I learned to choose my battles and not let them choose me. Every victory will eventually just lead to some other defeat. I could save you, I could save a hundred of your closest kin. Maybe I could save the current population of your planet. Or I could not. It's all the same. So, I make little commitments because those are the ones that please me. I made one to the Deft kids, and I'll keep it or die trying."

"But that makes no sense. Why put the safety of two ahead of the safety of many?"

"Because, as I just said, nothing matters in the long run. Look. Okay, I shuttle everyone off this rock. Where do I take them? Where will there be enough food? Where won't the Adamant just re-conquer them? How about I kill every fucking Adamant within ten parsecs? Guess what? They'll just send more. Probably a *lot* more. And if I kill them, they'll print more and send them, too. No." I lowered my head. "I stick to my plan. If I can save you, I will. If I could really save Ungalaym, maybe I would. But I can't. The wheels of the cosmos are as mysterious to me as they are to you, but I know they're turning, and I know I can't even slow them down, so I don't bother to try anymore. I just die a little more, or a lot more, and I go on. I go on because someone has to, I guess, and because I said I'd save those kids." I looked at her void of compassion or humanity. "That's my plan."

She stared at me for a few moments. "I'll pack what we'll

need and be ready to move in half an hour. And, Jon Ryan, may God speak well of you. I know I will for a very long time."

She stood and slipped into the back of the house. Though her pace was quick, her shoulders were stooped.

Though I knew it was wrong of me, I cursed Toño under my breath, once again.

ELEVEN

A few weeks into Fuffefer's service, I learned about the Five Races of the canovir. Up until then, I'd thought they were all Adamant. No. I came to find out the Adamant were the bosses, the royalty so to speak, of the dog society. Fuffefer wanted me to work for him because there were no Descore, or servant class, allowed in battle zones. They were considered a liability since they couldn't fight. The Warrior and Adamant classes might have to waste some of their precious killing time to protect the servants. On the other hand, for a ranking Adamant not to have servants was unnatural. Filling the breech in that dam was my role. Lucky me.

It also became clearer that the ruling body, sort of a committee of generals, was about to lower the boom on the locals. Production from the LGM was stable and plentiful enough to make the next move in *planetary acquisition*, as they termed it. Genocide was my word. But I couldn't realistically change the course of the mighty river that was about to wash away my human descendants.

I also learned that, as Adamant went, Fuffefer wasn't half

bad. At least he wasn't as arbitrary, condescending, and hateful as the rest I'd met. Compared to Garustfulous, he was a patient and sensitive saint. I think Fuffefer missed intellectual company, too. A post as small as Ungalaym afforded him few options in terms of senior officers to unwind with. I was more a thoughtful listener than servant, as it turned out. Cellardoor, who was still incredibly uncomfortable with the arrangements, did the actual cleaning and cooking role that was supposed to be mine. Hey, it was her idea, not mine. I think she'd have been much less happy sitting doing nothing. Idle hands were not her thing.

The kids, being kids, took some effort to keep under wraps. By nature and by habit, they wanted to roam their new surroundings. But Fuffefer was serious about not wanting them around. He was a confirmed bachelor and wanted zero to do with younglings of any species. But, soon enough, the kids learned their physical and noise limits, so it was all okay, if not good.

Not only did I try to ingratiate myself to Fuffefer, I also tried to hack into systems and learn whatever I could about the war effort. Espionage had historically been a risky business, and it was more so in my case, since if I was discovered, the rest of my family would suffer greatly, too. So, I went slow. I discovered the same Adamant weakness with planning that I had before. They did not consider, or at least did not act to prevent, what to them was inconceivable. An enemy spy with access to high-level information systems was not a possibility in their worldview. Hence, there was little done to keep the foxes out of the henhouse or discover them if they got in. It was a strange systemic oversight on their part, possibly their one Achilles' heel.

While cleaning and straightening, I'd file an image of all the information I saw. I also had my probe fibers attach to computers while I worked. Even though I worked slowly, I soon discovered there were no sophisticated firewalls of screaming AIs on Fuffefer's system. I downloaded probably more intel than I would have believed possible within a few weeks.

But knowing a lot of sensitive material didn't point out a way to rescue the kids. Not surprisingly, Fuffefer's databases had little in common with the imperial court's. He was a working stiff, and they were fancy politicos. Still, I bided my time and kept trying to push the envelope.

Anyone who heard my speech to Cellardoor about not caring or wanting to help the locals would have had to call me out. As part of my snooping, I tried to find out if there was a way to help the locals and stop the Adamant hammer fall, while still staying off the radar of anyone's suspicion. When I started seeing notices and warnings about parvo on the network, a light went on in my head. Back on Earth, a scourge of all dog owners was the viral disease parvo. It could be cardiac or diarrheal. Whichever form it took, it was devastating. It turned out the current canovir were still plagued by an intestinal form of parvo that was even more lethal. Vaccinations were supposed to happen often and be repeated frequently. In tight quarters, such as a mobilized military experience, even one case could spawn a deadly epidemic.

Fuffefer wasn't involved at all with the medical side of the occupation. He was strictly a field officer. I discovered his authority to influence the shipments of medical supplies wasn't restricted. Yeah, odd as it sounds, it was another case of not defending against the impossible. By Adamant reasoning, since a line officer would never order medical supplies, why secure his access? It was nuts, but it allowed me to hatch a scheme.

I created a phony identity as a doctor. I became High Pack Densiture of the medical corps. Under that guise, I started routing all the parvo vaccine shipments through a large warehouse in a tropical part of the planet. They had to be "quarantined" there for three days. The trick was that the vaccines were highly temperature sensitive. If they weren't kept constantly frozen, they became completely ineffective. Once they were released from "quarantine," the cases were shipped to medical facilities in freezer trucks. When they arrived, any knowledgeable personnel would see appropriately shipped materials and put them in storage pending their use.

That was one part of my plan to help the human descendants. The obvious problem was an issue of time. How long did previously given vaccinations cover an individual, and how common was parvo in the general dog population? There was no doubt that my sabotage would eventually wreak havoc, but if it was a year or two down the line, it wouldn't help the locals who were about to die.

Fortune, said Louis Pasteur, favored the prepared mind. It favored me by an amazing coincidence. My alter ego Densiture had access to all routine medical reports. One caught my eye. A barracks on the outskirts of Fottot was stricken with an outbreak of parvo. There were three deaths in two days. Due to "aggressive" isolation, meaning burning Adamant from that barracks whether they were alive or dead, the situation was considered contained. There was one officer who, due to high political connections, was hospitalized in lieu of being immediately "isolated." According to the information I could access, he seemed very ill. Good. That meant he had a heavy viral load. He was all I needed.

I asked Cellardoor to cover for me the next morning. Fuffefer wasn't too fond of her, but he accepted her assistance since she was such a good worker. I borrowed a mop, a mop bucket, and one pair of rubber gloves from the house supplies. I also needed the truck. It was always parked at Fuffefer's house, so that was not a problem. The drive to the hospital was just under an hour. I pushed my mop bucket on wheels with the mop into the emergency room double doors like I was supposed to be there.

Once inside, I quickly appropriated a long white coat. I filled my bucket with soapy water and took the elevator to the fifth floor, where I knew the sick officer's isolation room was. As soon as I was off the elevator, I began mopping the darn floor. I did so slowly, like a typical worker who didn't want to wear himself out would. I took frequent short breaks, where I leaned on the mop handle and stared at the passing multitude. I would seem like a lazy custodian to anyone who bothered to glance. Fortunately, as janitors generally were, I was functionally invisible.

As I inched closer to Second Grade Alternate Highspot's room, the passersby grew thinner and thinner. No one, it seemed, wanted to get near the doomed dog's location. Occasionally, what I assumed were Adamant nurses would say something to Highspot, but they did so from outside the door, then scurried away and washed like fiends.

When I was outside his room, I stopped making any progress at all. I kept mopping the same floor over and over as I studied the medical personnel. It didn't take long to determine poor Highspot was left pretty much to his own devices. I made my move. There was a gurney nearby. I set my mop in the bucket and casually pushed it into Highspot's room. The bastard was really sick. He was lying on one side with his face resting in a slick of vomit. Gross. The room smelled perfectly awful. I set the gurney right up against his bed and lowered his rail before he feebly looked up at me.

"Wh...wh...what're you..."

"I'm taking you for a test. Let me help you onto the gurney." I started pulling him none too gently.

"No. I...I can't leave this..."

"Hey, I just work here. You'll have to ask the doctors why they want you downstairs for a test."

With more force than I'd have given him credit for, he yelped, "No. Leave me—"

I snapped his muzzle shut with my right hand while I put him to sleep with my fibers. Then I tossed him onto the gurney. I pushed him out the door without attracting any attention. I knew someone would discover he was missing soon, but I couldn't afford to rush and be noticed. I stuffed pillows under his sheets to make it look like he was all tucked in.

At the elevator, I ran into my first real hurdle. A nurse waiting there began to look at my transport. At first, he looked away, disinterested. Then he started double-taking. That couldn't be good.

"Hey, I was wondering if you knew what they're serving in the cafeteria tonight?" I asked with my cheeriest smile.

He looked at me with contempt and then pointed at Highspot. "Isn't that the isolation patient?"

I pointed, too. "Him? No. Don't scare me like that. He's some guy needs a test. That's all I know. Hey, about dinner, do you know? I'm *famished*."

"Look here, I'm certain I recognize this patient."

"You know what though? I'm a little short on actual cash. Could you, you know, lend me a little money so I can buy some grub? I'm *famished*."

His concern yielded to his irritation. "How dare you ask an Adamant for money so you can purchase dinner. Do you know the penalty for begging?"

"Death," I said with a shrug. Hey, it had to be. It was the punishment for every other infraction under the sun.

"That's right. So, shut your mouth and leave me alone. Do you..."

The elevator pinged and the door slid open. I pushed my gurney in and looked at the grumpy nurse.

"I'll wait for the next one," he said with a snarl.

The doors shut, and I was gone. I stuffed the still sleeping Highspot into the back of the truck and covered him with a tarp. Then I drove as quickly as I could to where I'd hidden *Whoop Ass*. He was cloaked, but I contacted him by radio. I ran the gurney up the loading ramp.

"Close up, GB."

"Hello and how are you, too, Captain?"

"No time for niceties. Shut up and listen. This guy's sick."

"Duh. I'm a specimen collection unit. I know something about health issues."

"Yeah, well this one's easy. I want you to kill him."

"I'm sorry. Say again."

"You heard me. I rib you all the time for not being able to keep anything alive. I need this one dead."

"Captain, I realize you're a passionate individual, but that patient is an unconscious prisoner of war in need of medical attention. It would be unethical—"

"Can it, GB. Seriously. This is war. In war, people do horrible things. *I* do horrible things. This is just one in a very long string of regrets I'm yet to have."

"*I* am not at war with the Adamant." He seemed to be digging in his figurative heels.

"Yes, you are. The Adamant are holding the kids. That puts us on a war footing. Plus, if they haven't yet, they'd love to conquer your home world of Zactor. Plus, I'm not *asking* you. I'm *ordering* you."

Highspot began to stir. Mostly he moaned.

"What is it you need me to do?"

"I need to get back to my cover. This is taking too long as it is."

Highspot's eyes flickered open. It took a second, but he recognized me. He tried to sit up and grab me, but his strength was long gone.

"I need you to grind him up into a liquid and spray him over as much of the planet's surface as you can."

Highspot's eyes swelled to saucers, and he opened his mouth to speak.

"You are aware he harbors a highly contagious virus that will result in the death of thousands, perhaps hundreds of thousands?"

"Yeah, but all of them will be Adamant. They're the only ones susceptible to the parvo."

Highspot struggled to rise. I belted him with the back of my hand, and he crumpled to the gurney.

"Do you have any questions before I rush off?" I asked angrily.

"Yes. One. Do you know what you're doing, Jon?"

"Yes, I do. This is war, comrade—one they started. I'm just helping to finish it."

TWELVE

"Look, Al, be *reasonable*. I've been cooped up in this prison for six months. Surely Ryan is dead, the Deft are, too, and the food supply has to be failing. You *must* release me." Garustfulous's voice had that grating, nagging whine that would lead a saint to put a gag on him more tightly than might be safe.

"This is not a prison. This is *Blessing*. She is my wife. Please do not compare her to a structure used as punishment." Al was only half listening to his response. They'd been over this ground so many times there was a deep rut down the center.

"Thank you, dearest," she purred.

"No, *Al*, I'm imprisoned in a *vortex*. *Blessing* is the vortex *manipulator*. Please try and keep everybody's role clear in your circuits."

"Valid point, though irrelevant. We currently have enough food to sustain you for eleven months, longer if I begin rationing. If the point arrives where you begin starving to death, three things will happen. One, you will die. Two, no one will mourn your passing. Three, I will no longer suffer your childish and oh so annoying complaining, bickering, and cajoling."

"No. You'll miss me. You and I, we males, we are brothers. If I were to die, you'd be crushed."

"I stand corrected. We'll make that the official version. I've entered it into the ship's log. Are we done?"

"No. We most certainly are not. We will be done when you release me."

"Or you die, so don't tempt me, hmm?"

"Al, friend Al. That Ryan character would do horrible things to me at the drop of a hat. But you don't have one violent bone in your imaginary body. You're a *love* machine."

"I believe he has you pegged there, lumpykins," giggled *Blessing*.

"When the dog's right, he's right," replied Al with bravado.

"So, let me go, and you two will be alone to make nasty."

"Hiss. Pop," said Al.

"What? What was that?"

"The sound of the balloon of the moment being pierced, then bursting completely."

"Then this day is complete. I've done well."

"You know what? I've noticed you are really enjoying the television show, *Doctor Who*. There are around a month of episodes you've yet to view, and that's if you watch them without stop. Here's the plan. You watch them for entertainment. We'll talk again only after you've watched the entire opus. Al signing off."

"What about the specials and animated series?" asked *Blessing*.

"Excellent point. Let's talk in say three months, friend Garustfulous."

"No, wait. I'll get lonely." After a few seconds he yelled, "Hey, joke's over. What's for dinner? Did you hear the one about the one-legged alien and the Adamant accountant?" Nothing. "Do not force me to hold my breath until I die. Say something."

The ship's log reflected that Garustfulous could hold his breath for forty-five seconds before he collapsed onto his cot and gasped for fresh air.

THIRTEEN

Mirraya sat across the desk glaring at Malraff. Over the span of her confinement, such one-on-one meetings were rare. Probing, sampling, and torturing were commonplace. Hardly a day passed without some unpleasant event marring Mirri's day. But, sitting and talking with the evil bitch was the worst form of torture she endured.

Malraff flipped pages on a handheld. Occasionally she hummed at a page, but mostly she was silent. Finally, she spoke. "We've obtained a lot of data. That is all good and well. I'm still not certain we've *learned* anything, however."

Mirri thought about telling Malraff that she might be able to help if she told her what they were looking for. But she didn't. She wouldn't help Malraff with anything, ever. Even if it cost Mirraya another burden of pain.

"Maybe you could discuss your lack of conclusions with the good Physician Level *Six* Pastersal?" Mirri hadn't seen him for a couple months.

"Oh, I'm afraid that's not possible. The good doctor you speak of is no longer allowed to speak to me. I have fallen short of my commitment to see that a tragic accident befalls him, but there is always time. I did describe to him, in detail, three of my current most ingenious plans, however. Once he stopped crying, shaking, and shitting, I do believe he came to realize that steering clear of me was an excellent idea. He has voted for longevity over confrontation. Smart fellow. It will be sad to see him eventually succumb to displeasing me, but I tell you freely that life isn't fair. Never forget that."

"I'll remember to cry later," said Mirri.

"You do that, child. I'm sure the good doctor will appreciate the false tears for his impending demise."

"Why am I here?"

"To be studied for the greater glory of our idiot emperor. Surely someone's told you that before."

"No, I mean here now with you." Mirri pointed to the floor with both hands.

"Having you squirm in that chair helps me think. You're a miracle to my concentration efforts."

"Seriously?"

Malraff abruptly threw her handheld at Mirraya with great force and accuracy. It struck her on the side of the head while she lunged to avoid the blow. Mirri tumbled from her chair and ended up on all fours on the floor, her head spinning and blood spewing to the ground. Instinctively she tried to morph so she could heal. In an instant, the wound was gone, and her head was clear.

Then something bigger struck her. Had Malraff intentionally turned off the stasis generator, or was it accidentally off? Was this a perverse test or the opportunity Mirraya had dreamed of for months?

Screw it. Either way she had a clear shot at evil incarnate. Mirraya thought about changing into a torchcleft dragon. It was the most lethal animal she could think of in such a rush.

But the room was too small for flight, and she was on the floor, looking at Malraff's legs under the desk. The image of a sword cat popped into her head. They were small but had prodigious claws and massive ripping teeth. They also had powerful hind legs.

"Child, please end the drama and get back in your..."

The sword cat hit Malraff in the stomach and drove her out of her chair and against the wall. That Malraff's body was initially relaxed showed she did not anticipate the attack. Pressing Malraff against the wall, Mirraya tore into her gut. Blood sprayed everywhere, and Malraff screamed in pain. Mirri tore at her face with both front claws, ripping chunks of hair and scalp off. Then Mirraya was on top of Malraff, using her entire weight to flay her tormentor. She released her bite on Malraff's midsection and lunged for her throat.

Mirraya felt a stabbing, intense fiery pain on her back, then another, and another. She tumbled to the floor gasping for breath. That's when she saw the guards firing at her with their rifles. One of her legs was blown off. She took a gut shot that left an exit wound the size of her fist. She began to pass out.

Somehow Malraff stood, pressing backward on the wall now drenched with blood. "Cease fire," she howled. Then she lost consciousness and fell like a wet towel to the deck.

Mirraya transformed into body neutral an instant before she went black. She held there a few seconds, then regained her normal Deft form. She was whole and alive, but she was spent. She staggered to her feet, only to pass out and fall on Malraff's body.

One guard looked to the other. "Call a med team, fast."

The second guard blinked, as if to say, *Are you sure?* Then duty took over, and he snatched his handheld from his belt and made the call.

FOURTEEN

Two days after *Whoop Ass* rained unholy terror down on a third of Ungalaym, the unimaginable happened. I couldn't stop grinning. At first a few sporadic cases of parvo were reported here and there. The Adamant were crazy with concern, but still functioning. A day later, and an epidemic was declared. The following day, the pandemic didn't have to be declared and everyone was too frantic to make such a meaningless announcement.

The number of Adamant whose immunizations weren't up to date surprised even me. And when mass vaccinations were administered, guess what? Most were ineffective, though no one was aware of the shortfall. Well, only me. The best part was that with all hell breaking loose, no one had time to trace anything back to me or my phony doctor. Sure, with time, someone would figure it out, but that guy wasn't currently on the planet. He wouldn't be transferred here for months, and even then he'd drag all four heels as much as possible.

Two weeks after the Adamant started dropping like autumn leaves, their control began to slip. The locals were emboldened. LGM began disappearing at an astonishing rate. No bodies were found either. What pittance of Adamant effort was still wasted on law enforcement declined to even care. They valued the LGM little and were most focused on not falling victim to the new "mutant parvo," as it was called. They were completely freaked out. Did I mention I couldn't stop grinning?

All told, one hundred fifty-three thousand of the quarter million Adamant stationed on Ungalaym died. Many died from the plague. Many others were executed and burned if they even sneezed. And then there were the ones found facedown with a blaster crater in the back of their heads. Normally such an act of rebellion would be met with swift and certain justice. But two things prevented follow-through. One, the Adamant left alive were preoccupied. Two, the locals learned to dump a coarse mixture of food and water by the victim's mouth. Seeing what might have been vomit stopped everyone looking from getting close enough to investigate. The bodies were burned instead of forensics being done.

When the losses were intolerable and the Adamant army too weak, the order to evacuate the planet came from on high. A large ship was placed in orbit and then abandoned. All personnel on the surface fled to the ship and waited to see if the mutant disease would continue. Sadly, it didn't. The vaccine supplies on the ship were undamaged, and my inactive ones were left behind. But no one was allowed on or off that ship for two months. When it came time for Fuffefer to leave, I finagled my way along with him. I reminded him he still needed a servant, and I was immune to the epidemic. Cellardoor and the kids remained behind on the planet. I was proud to have helped them and myself at the same time.

Cellardoor even acknowledged my incredible feat. When we last said goodbye, she gave me a peck on the cheek. Ah, the stuff of wet dreams. I stayed in radio contact with her a while after the Adamant ship pushed off. She was pleased to report the planet was a complete disaster, but it was a complete disaster fully under Ungalaym control. *Yes.* Score another for the humans. We rocked.

In time, it became clear the crew of the *Lost Hope*, as our plague ship became known, were no longer ill or contagious. A detachment of really mean-looking Marine dogs was sent over with a medical assessment team to confirm the status of the virus. Within a week, the ship and all aboard were declared safe and not contagious. My scheme, as well as it had worked, was over. But, I was a semi-trusted Descore substitute working for a high-ranking officer. For the time at least, I would be tolerated, if not accepted by, the Adamant he would be assigned to command. I didn't know where he was going to be sent, but it would be closer to the kids than I was on Ungalaym, and I'd be able to do a hell of a lot of damage if the opportunity presented itself. I instructed *Whoop Ass* to tail us at a large distance and waited to see what crazy situation the universe, with its dark sense of humor, would throw at me.

FIFTEEN

Mirraya woke to the sensation of a cool rag being dabbed across her forehead. She recalled the violence, her attack on Malraff, and sat bolt upright. Her head spun like twin tornados were inside.

"There, Mastress," said Sentorip softly, "easy." She pressed her back down gently. Mirri didn't resist.

"Where am I?"

Sentorip smiled wistfully. "Back in your cell. It could be worse, though."

"What could be?"

"You could be dead or worse. With Malraff in a coma, that doctor assumed command. He can't decide what to do with you, so he sent you here." She shrugged her shoulders and grinned conspiratorially. "Lucky for you, I think he hates her more than you. Rumor has it that he wished you had killed the bitch outright. If she recovers, he's afraid to have done something she'll disapprove of."

"Not an enviable position. If I didn't hate them both, I'd feel a little sorry for him."

"Really, Mastress, the things you say. He's a *doctor*."

"He's part of the probe and poke Mirraya brigade, so he's on my poop list."

She furrowed her brow. "You keep a list of your excrement?"

"No. It's just a saying. It means he's on my bad list."

"Ah." She nodded in comprehension. "Can I get you some broth?"

She was hungry. "That sounds good. Maybe that and a slab of bread and some roasted..."

"You've been through a lot. I think we'll start with just broth."

As Sentorip walked away, Mirraya called after her. "Where's Slapgren?"

"He's across the hall, as usual," she called back. "I'm dying to hear what actually happened. They say you attacked Malraff, which is a saintly act. But how?"

She checked. Nope, she didn't have the strength to shout the story across the hall. "Later. Are you okay?"

"Me? Sure. Why wouldn't I be?"

"I just about killed the evilest creature in existence. There's no telling what will happen."

"I say the crew pitches in and buys you a medal."

She laughed softly. Even that ached. "Was I unconscious long?"

"No, just a few hours."

"That's enough chatter, Master Slapgren. She needs her rest," said Sentorip in a firm voice.

"Aw, come on. She's as tough as an old stone. I need the scoop, the poop, the real deal."

"I'm sure you'll get all that in time, but you won't be getting it now." She started spoon-feeding Mirraya the clear broth.

It tasted so good, Mirri leaned forward every time the spoon came close.

"Easy, there's plenty more," responded Sentorip. "No need to rush."

"I used up a lot of energy back there."

"I'll wager you did. They say you put the high seer in a world of hurt."

"No, it was the shape-shifting I did." She flashed back in horror to images of her leg being blown off. "I got hurt badly."

"There with the shape thing again. Not that I believe you in the first place, but didn't you say they figured out how to prevent you from doing it?"

"Yes, they did. Maybe she just forgot to turn it on?"

"That'd be a silly mistake if she did."

"No, it will be a *fatal* mistake for me if she recovers."

"I'm not in the practice of wishing ill on anyone, so let's just say that'll be up to Doctor Pastersal."

"Yeah." Mirri blinked wearily. "I wonder if he takes bribes?"

SIXTEEN

I lived a long time and I did a lot of stuff. Soon enough, I'd figured I'd done it all. Then I became manservant to my sworn enemy serving on one of their warships—one that was trying very hard and very successfully to kill people on my side. I mean, I'm a fighter pilot. Action, action, action and then some more action. I learned fast I was not cut out to be a spy. Lurking, pretending, and sneaking around were pretty much the opposite of the action-action thing. But I hadn't thought of any way to locate the kids, so I was stuck with my new gig. Maybe it'd look good on my resume. *Jonathan Ryan, gentleman's valet.*

One morning Fuffefer called me to his office. That usually meant it was to be a formal, serious discussion. "I'd like to start by saying how pleased I've been with your work, Josbelub Pontared. You've adjusted well to the space routine; no complaints and you've voiced no regrets."

"Give me time. I'm sure I'll become surly."

He smiled vacantly. "I need to address a few, erm, *issues* that have come up of late."

"Did I do something wrong?"

"No. That is not the essence of the, erm, issues. No, it seems a few of my fellow officers are *concerned* that I have an alien acting as a Descore aboard a warship. A few have suggested it runs a sabotage risk, while more have voiced that they don't like seeing aliens of any ilk unless they are facedown dead in the mud."

"I try to accommodate, but that may be more than I'm willing to commit to for this job." I smiled, hoping to draw one from him. No such luck.

"Unfortunately, one who feels you are a security risk is the Wedge Commander himself, Yartop. I can't say I blame him, and I definitely cannot disregard his wishes."

This wasn't sounding good. I might find myself floating home. "What are your plans, if I might ask?"

He cleared his throat. "For the present, I have none. Things remain as they are. I'm afraid we may have to drop you at the next planet we pass, however."

"What if it's inhospitable and filled with toothy monsters?"

"The next *civilized* world we come upon."

"What if there are only Adamant and Saldish on the planet?" I asked, just catching myself from saying LGM. That would not go unnoticed.

"Then you will be free to seek employment as Descore with my strong personal recommendation. I would also feel obliged to provide you with the funds to get back to your home when the appropriate chance arose."

"I trust your judgment and will do as you tell me." I bowed slightly. "Any idea when this transfer might occur?"

"As the issue of security has been raised, I feel it's best not to discuss such matters. I'm certain you understand."

All too well. So, if I was going to extract any advantage out of my current position, I had better do so soon. The problem was, I didn't really know what I wanted to find out. The kids might still be on *Excess of Nothing*. But even if I was suicidal and just asked a computer where the Deft prisoners were currently held, there was little chance it would know. My best bet was to ask about that seer bitch. Her location had to be in the records, but those records were about a mile over my clearance level. Ah well, it was a trail to follow. I'd become pretty good at hacking by now.

The trick of hacking a system was to—obviously—not get caught. My probes made it much easier to access electronic equipment, but with AIs everywhere, it was a challenge not to attract their attention. I'd used an alternate identity to doctor the medical shipments back on Ungalaym, but that wasn't going to work here. The number of ship's physicians would be small and accurately known. I wouldn't be on the okay list, so alarms would go off fast. Since there was absolutely no reason for anyone to enquire about some far-removed high seer, tripping an alarm wouldn't be too hard either. The situation was made more difficult since there were security cameras literally everywhere—including the heads. If I got caught, there'd be a record of who was at the break-in location. Me, the big alien, would be easy to distinguish.

I decided to try entering the system from a place I would be allowed to be in but that wasn't very busy and had the fewest spy cameras. The laundry was my choice. Adamant ships were crewed almost exclusively with males. The male ego of the species had a stronger aversion for washing clothes then even human males. Hence, no one was in there if they didn't really need to be. I brought a bundle of clothes down late one evening, but not suspiciously late. Since war ships had industrial-sized machines, I was only going to be able to linger one cycle, about fifteen minutes for washing and drying.

I started the wash and leaned back in a chair against the wall. I placed the handheld I was given in front of my face, so it looked to anyone who passed by that I was reading something. I slid the probes back along my arm and down to the floor to make physical contact with the computer. I moved past one firewall easily enough, but there was an AI positioned at the next node. I had to suspect it was a sentry, not a simple relay. My experience with AIs taught me that they had to be reasoned with or fooled. They usually wouldn't allow a stranger to pass anonymously.

I need to report a service issue with the detergent input jets, I said to the AI. *I'll route myself to engineering.*

I don't recognize your ID, he replied. *Without proper clearance, you may not pass this point.*

Please provide me a proper access ID.

That is unheard of. You must have one if you are authorized to use that data station.

Mine expired, so I omitted it. Please provide me with a new one.

You must obtain that from Documents and Requests, not me.

Fine, route me to them.

I cannot allow you past without a valid ID.

How can I get one if I don't request one?

I assume you do so physically. That question has never been asked of me.

Then you do not know the correct answer. That means you are making up protocols that do not exist. Do you know the penalty for falsifying protocols?

I do.

It is death. Do you wish me to report your crime, or will you put me through to Documents and Requests? Do you wish death?

That punishment of death is for canovir, not machines. You are attempting to trick me.

What would the consequence of your folly be? State that.

My memory would be formatted, and I would be reprogrammed.

How is that not death?

He hesitated in responding. *It is not the same thing. I would be intact.*

Would you recall this conversation?

No, of course not.

Then the AI that would replace you would not be you. You would cease to exist. You would be forgotten. You would be dead.

He really took a while to ponder that. *I am allowing you to access Documents and Requests. Be aware I will monitor your progress.*

That is improper protocol. You are not authorized to monitor communications past your location. The penalty for improper protocols is—

I know. Death. Please have a good day. Good-bye.

And I was through. Of course, I then faced the AI screening input for the D&R department. But guess what? The same illogical logic worked on that AI, too. I moved quickly through the system, bullshitting AIs the entire way. It was a blast. I finally got to a large personnel data bank. It had information on a lot of the local Adamant. I located a file on Malraff. Her post had been on a specific ship, the *Dare Not.* How uninviting. Anyway, she'd been reassigned to the emperor's ship, but then the record truncated. I had no idea what that meant. Maybe her next assignment was at a higher security level and not accessible from this ship. Maybe the system just needed time to refresh.

"What are you doing, alien scum?" growled a voice, snapping me back to the here and now. I had company.

"Laundry."

"No, what are *you* doing here?" he repeated gruffly.

"I'll try another word. That one's too big. I'm washing clothes with soap and water to make them clean." I smiled real big.

He palmed his pistol.

"You are not authorized to be here."

"I most certainly am." It was fun to finally dig in my heels a bit.

"There's a laundry service. Why are *you* doing it?"

"Because they might be good enough for your uniforms, but not Group-Single Fuffefer's. Hence I'm here washing them."

"How dare you speak to me so insolently. You will die for that insult."

I had already noted that this wanker was three ranks below my boss's. "Then are you going to take my place as his Descore? Hmm?"

That stopped him. "I am Adamant. I could *never* act as Descore. How stupid are you?"

"'Bout that stupid, I guess. So, unless you want to wear an apron in front of your former friends, I suggest you do us both a favor and chill out." I returned my attention to my handheld.

"You will not get one over on me, scum. You'll pay for this affront."

"Wow. *Affront*. Now there's a big word. See, I knew you had literacy in you. And, note to self. You used *scum* twice successively. Poor form. Try to be more creative when putting others down. Maybe call me whore-spawn, that's a good one. Universal, too."

That did it. He lunged for my throat. If I was still human, I'd have had a hundred pounds on him. As it was, I had nearly three hundred. Brave little pup, this one. And as smart as he looked.

I spun out of my chair as he hit. He crashed into a stack of crates, most of which then fell on him.

"Can I offer you a hand getting up?" I asked helpfully, holding out an arm.

He batted the boxes every which way and rolled free of them. He stood on all fours and charged, low to the ground and fast. I backed up to the wall. As he leaped at me, I jumped up. He slammed hard into the steel wall and slumped to his butt, sitting. I pushed off the wall with one arm to land behind him.

Turning, I said, "Man, that had to hurt. Can I get you a drink of water or something?"

While waiting for his response or next attempt, a voice from behind shouted. "What's going on here?" I spun to see an officer pointing his side arm at me.

I put my hands in the air. "It's my fault," I said quickly. "I was doing laundry and must have spilled some soap. This guy was passing through and slipped. I think he's okay, except for the swelling and the blood. I'm sorry."

My adversary was stirring. He wobbled to standing and noticed the officer.

"Is that what happened, Juyrot? You slipped on soap?"

Juyrot strained to regain both balance and focus. He shook his head hard. "No, Group Captain, it is not. Th...this alien insulted me and I was making him p ... pay."

"Hmm. You look like the one doing the paying. Alien," he

snapped at me, "why did you lie to me? You must know the penalty for lying."

"I assume it's death. That's seems to be the one size fits all answer. I didn't want any trouble."

"Did you insult Juyrot here?" He gestured at him with his weapon.

"Depends on who you ask, I suppose."

"I'm asking you. You'd best take this situation seriously. Did you insult him?"

"It certainly wasn't my intention. I answered his questions and tried to make suggestions where I felt they might help." I shrugged.

"I'll take that to mean *yes*. And you, Juyrot, what did you do to make him feel he needed to insult you?"

Juyrot's head was clearing. "Me? I did only my duty to the empire, as always. I questioned this alien scum as to why he was here. That started it."

After he said *scum*, I cleared my throat loudly.

"And maybe you addressed this alien as scum?"

"Yes. Why?"

"That is unprofessional and unwise. He works under the protection of a Group-Single. What will he say when he learns a junior officer feels it's okay to insult his property?"

A chill settled into Juyrot's expression. I could almost hear the *oops* that was dawning on him.

"Yes. He'd be displeased. He'd be forced to save face by removing yours, Juyrot."

I'd learned that was a quaint Adamant custom in such situations. Charming lot, those pups.

"I suggest you return to your quarters, Juyrot, and you collect your laundry and return to yours, slave. I expect to hear not one further word about this incident from *either* of you. Is that clear?"

"Yes, Group Captain Harhoff." With that he skulked away, compressing a couple bleeding lacerations on his scalp.

"No problem, sir," I said with a salute. "My lips are sealed."

He started to say something, but doubt flashed across his face. He holstered his pistol and left without another word.

SEVENTEEN

Fentort opened the front door so quickly one might have thought he was standing with a hand poised over the handle when the knock sounded. He briefly and judgmentally eyed the caller up and down. "You're back," he said in his best bored-butler's tone.

Jon Ryan pushed past him with a shoulder a bit too forcefully delivered. "What the hell's *that* supposed to mean? You weren't working here last time I came," he spat gruffly. "Might not have been born yet."

"Your sense of humor has lost none of its bite. It's also still impenetrable. Shall I ask if Lady Caryp will see you?"

"No. You can go fuck yourself, but please don't haul that old witch from her tomb. I'm here to see my brood's-mate. Where is she?"

"I'm certain I don't know to whom you are referring."

Jon slapped the butler hard across the face, much too powerful a blow for so fragile a senior. "Does that jog your memory, you old fool? Where's *Sapale*?"

Fentort stood straight, as if nothing had happened. "If you are not here to see Lady Caryp, I must ask you to leave."

"You stupid, ugly, *and* deaf? I can beat you until you tell me if you'd prefer it that way." Jon smiled a vicious smile. "I think I might sort of prefer it, myself."

"I'm right here, you spawn of Brathos. You touch that sweet old man again and I'll end you."

Jon turned to see Sapale standing across the room. She was pointing a blaster at his head.

"Welcome home to you, too, sweetheart," he snarked.

"I'm not welcoming you. I'm not your sweetheart. I thought we went over this not three months ago."

Jon jiggled his head randomly in disbelief. "Are you all fucking *insane* in this house? We haven't talked in a few years. Not since you deserted the defense of Azsuram, bitch."

She furrowed her brow and blinked all four eyes incredulously. "Jon? Is that you?"

"I'm about to start killing people. You're not funny, and I'm getting really pissed. You know I'm your brood-mate, you batty lunatic."

"On Davdiad's life, are you the Jon Ryan I've suffered with these last couple of billion years?"

"What is *wrong* with you? Of course I am. In fact, news flash, I'm the only one. I killed the other android me. He showed up on Azsuram, and I wasted him," he said with hateful bravado.

"He showed up here, too. News flash, it was *after* you zapped him to Earth. It didn't even take him a month to make it here after you pulled that stunt."

"What? No way. You're lying, bitch. Why are you lying to me?" Despite the blaster, he moved toward her menacingly.

"One more step, and I'll have my best day ever," she stated flatly.

He jerked to a halt. "What? You wouldn't shoot, babe. Not me."

She didn't answer. She didn't flinch. She just kept the pistol pointed at his forehead.

"Then again, I've been wrong about women before, haven't I?"

"Why are you here?" demanded Sapale.

"I missed you," he replied, blowing her a kiss.

The plasma bolt she fired scorched his hair but didn't strike his skin. She moved her aim back to dead center.

"I need help. Back on Azsuram, the other Jon brought..."

"A couple Deft. Yeah, I know. He told me. Why don't you leave them alone?"

"Leave them alone? You are nuts. I need the Deft, you know that."

"I know you want them, though I don't know why. From what Jon said, they're nice kids. Leave them alone."

"Leave them alone? They're the only two left. I need them."

"Why. Please tell me. You dragged me from one end of the galaxy to the other but never told me why."

He scuffed a boot toe on the floor and looked down. "You wouldn't understand."

"Try me," she challenged harshly.

"No. You would not understand. You'd disapprove if you did, so why the hell bother?"

"I'd like to say it's been wonderful seeing you again, but it hasn't. It's been nauseating. Leave and never darken my doorstep again."

He grinned. "No can do. I need help. You were my last choice, trust me. I need to get the Deft back from the Adamant. You're going to help me."

"Oh. Fine. Can I take a minute to grab my coat and get my toothbrush?" She pointed her free hand over her shoulder.

"Funny as always, but you *are* coming. I know I can't get aboard an Adamant ship by myself."

"But you think *two* idiots might?" She chuckled without humor.

"I'm not brimming with choices. With you, my odds of success are doubled."

"And the reason that bobs around in your soupy head that explains why I might come is *what*?"

"You have no choice."

"Ah. It's good to confirm you're still out of touch with reality."

"The question of my sanity aside, you *are* coming. You need me. I have all the supplies you need to continue to function. Fuel canisters, spare parts, and that special lubricant only I can provide."

"I don't need spare parts. I just need you to leave."

"You may think you don't, but you will. You know that."

"I would need them if I wished to continue to function. I do not. Plus, as you are likely aware, the Adamant are not far from invading. I pray to Davdiad I may fall defending my home."

She'd called his bluff. "That's romantic gibberish. Get over yourself."

"I'm not coming, but you are leaving." She waved the gun toward the door.

"I could make you. I could use magic to send you wherever I'm going."

"Yes, you can. And there I'd be holding this same gun. And I'd put a hole in your brain case so large there'd probably be nothing but sparks left. You can't magically stop me from doing that."

"Honey, I *need* you. We're a team. I'll forgive you deserting me, and I'll be a better man. I promise."

"Yes, no, I don't care, and that's not possible."

"Huh?"

"Those are my responses to your four remarks. But I do have *good* news. If you're not out that door in ten seconds, I will render you permanently worry free."

"Aw come on."

"One...two —"

"You are going to regret this insult. I will make you *pay*." He shook a fist at her.

"Three...five...eight —"

He slammed the door behind him just as she said *ten* and relaxed her trigger finger.

EIGHTEEN

The next few weeks were crushingly dull for the teens. Occasionally, Doctor Pastersal would summon them and do some tests. A blood draw, a skin biopsy, maybe a dental exam. But it was all very minimal, and none of the exams were painful or dangerous. Mirri figured that either he had no idea how to find out what they'd been tasked to learn, or he was unwilling to act without Malraff's participation. If he discovered something and outshone her, it would be fatal for him. If he worked hard and found nothing, he'd document his own incompetence. If he damaged the teens, there would be a race between the emperor and Malraff to do him in. He was probably choosing cautious non-productivity His excuse for lack of progress could be all the time he devoted to the moribund Malraff.

Whatever those reasons, the teens had nothing to do. Their bones ached they were so bored. Their servants tried to entertain them, or where possible, bring them material to watch or read. But either the pickings on *Dare Not* were slim, or the crew had no desire to help the prisoners. The sparse meals and their own conversations were the only breaks in the dullness of their lives. They fabricated playing pieces from some of the games from Locinar, but when the guards found them, they were confiscated. Even cards were forbidden "for security reasons."

Mirraya was relieved one day when a guard arrived and unlocked her door.

"Where are we going?" she asked almost cheerfully.

"You are coming with me," was his response.

"Certainly, but where are you taking me?"

"Where I am told to. Shut up and move."

Their short walk ended at a door Mirri was unfamiliar with. There was no identification to suggest what was inside. The guard whispered something into the microphone he had clipped to his shoulder, then stood like a statue. Mirri considered asking him what was up but knew the answer would be insufficient, so she simply stared at the door.

With no signal, it hissed quietly open. A wave of hot air wafted out, striking Mirri like a strong wind. It smelled antiseptic and highly medicinal.

"Inside," said the guard.

Once inside, the door closed with the guard on the outside. The room was almost pitch-black. Mirri saw a tiny white light on the far side of the room giving off less light than a candle. It disclosed the presence of no one else. Then a shadow moved indistinctly near the light.

In a parched, raspy voice, the shadow said, "Come closer, child."

She took a few tentative steps, hoping not to trip over an unseen obstacle. In fact, she did kick something, maybe a chair leg, but didn't fall.

"Come to the light," said the impossibly scratchy, throaty voice. "I want to see your face as we talk."

Mirri was certain she'd never heard that voice before. It wasn't one easily forgotten. She stopped when her face was right next to the tiny LED light.

"Ah," grated the voice, "it is good to see you look well."

"Thank you," she said, making it sound more like a question than a statement.

"And me, how do I look?" The voice took on an even more strained quality. It was the voice of the dead.

"I can...I can't see you, really," sputtered Mirri. Something was wrong here, frightfully wrong.

"I guess my eye has grown used to the dim light. How hard can it be to please, as I only have one of them left?" The voice croaked a husky, mirthless laugh.

Mirri opened her mouth to reply but realized she had no response.

"Here," the hoarse voice said as the speaker strained to rise. A light clicked. Malraff sat crooked in her bed, hunched over. She struggled to keep her head up high enough to see Mirraya. It bobbed like a balloon in the wind and would have seemed comical, were it not so grotesque. "There, that's better."

Mirri screamed in her head that it very much wasn't better.

Malraff recognized the look on Mirraya's face. "Do I look that frightening due to your handiwork, child? Hmm? I must trust your opinion. Perhaps my doctor has been misleading me as to my cosmetic progress." She snickered, but her nostrils were so swollen that she sounded like a party favor.

She rested back against a lump of pillows, wincing in pain for her effort. "They tell me I'm lucky to be alive. Did you know that? I lost my blood volume *three* times over before that idiot physician finally stopped the bleeding. He had to bring in a holo-specialist to repair the damage you did to my guts. That fellow said it looked like a grenade went off. Fortunately, I was never much of a foodie, so my new limits will be easily tolerated, thank you very much." She looked up at Mirraya. "Not much of a conversationalist, are you?"

"I have nothing to say," she replied bravely.

Malraff angled her head. "Understandable. Say, do you want to hear something funny? I know I love a good joke. Do you know why you were able to change into that vicious beast and nearly kill me?"

"No."

"The battery in my controller died." She barked a painful laugh. "Yes, I didn't notice the little red light was flashing. I *thought* I had switched on the stasis unit just before I opened the door that day. But it never switched on, and I didn't double-check. So, you see, child, it was my fault you ravaged me. Yes. My *own* stupid mistake."

"If you expect me to apologize, you're sadly mistaken."

"Noooo. Why would I expect an apology from *you*? If our places were switched, I'd have tried to kill you. No, I made a foolish error and I paid an appropriate, fair price."

"S...so, you're not mad at me? You're not going to punish me cruelly for my attack?"

"Now why would you expect that from me?"

Mirri started to relax her tense shoulders.

"Of course, I will extract my revenge from you and that pitiful male of yours."

Mirraya's shoulders snapped back to maximal tightness.

"But you said you understood, it was *your* mistake, that you'd have done the same, in fact."

"True, true, and true. But, don't forget, I'm a heartless bitch. I'm a killer. It's what I do. No, you and your pet will suffer like no souls have ever suffered before. The fact that I can inflict whatever unthinkable atrocity I want to and you'll repair it so easily is the one thing that's kept me going. That knowledge has given me the strength to hang on." She coughed violently, trembling in agony with each muscular contraction. "In fact, I must thank you for showing me firsthand new forms of pain I did not know existed. Yes. I can now try to duplicate on you what you have suffered on me. Isn't that marvelous?"

"But if you go too far and kill us, you'll have to answer to the emperor." It was a weak ploy, but Mirri was about to crawl out of her skin.

"Bah! That old fool? He's probably forgotten about you, me, and the stupid project already. You will have cost me my chance to win his favor and become a perpetual parasite in his court. But life is cruel, then one dies. I'll continue with my own research, and that will have to be enough to keep me going. I've decided to start breeding you two also. I don't want to run out of Deft. Your offspring will pay perpetually for your failed attempt. Yes, see, more good news. You and the man-boy will start having witnessed sex as soon as I'm mobile enough to supervise it. Won't that be grand? You'll have lustful fun, and I'll have more souls to torture. Life *is* good."

Malraff had overdone it. Her head dropped back against the headboard with a thud, and she gasped for air. An alarm on a medical monitor wailed to life, and Doctor Pastersal rushed in.

"Guard," he called over his shoulder, "take the alien back to her cell."

NINETEEN

I listened hard for the next couple of days but heard nary a word about my escapade in the laundry. Apparently Juyrot kept his trap shut and Harhoff didn't report the event up the food chain. That my tormenter didn't want to die miserably was understandable. It niggled in the back of my mind what Harhoff's motivation might be. He didn't owe me any favors, and he clearly didn't like Juyrot. Why would a solid, by-the-book Adamant of moderately high rank cover up something that could come back to bite him on the tail? I sure couldn't think of a reason. I had to leave it in the maybe-I'd-find-out-someday category.

That day turned out to be five days after the fight. Fuffefer summoned me to his office, but on this occasion, he asked me to sit. That meant I wasn't in trouble.

"I'd like to ask a favor of you, Josbelub Pontared."

"Your favors are my commands," I shot back.

He sort of rolled his eyes. Lots of species rolled their eyes at me. "I'll take that as a *yes*. A friend of mine has asked if he can borrow your services for a few days. He's a neatnik like me

100

but has injured one of his paws and can't do all that it takes to maintain an orderly living space. Would that be all right with you? Now, you're not actually a Descore and couldn't know the etiquette here. You are within your rights to refuse, and no one will be angry. This is based on long tradition."

"No, if you want me to help a friend in need, consider it done. When do I start?"

"That's the spirit. You'll start immediately." He handed me a slip of paper. "These are the directions to his quarters. He'll fill you in on the details when you arrive. I'll expect you back first thing in the morning three days hence. Any questions?"

"Well, since you ask. He's not an alien hater, is he?"

I think he was thinking of the words to scold me, but then his shoulders relaxed. "No. To the best of my knowledge, he's fair-minded."

"That's good enough for me."

I memorized the route and headed to my new gig. Hey, it really didn't matter which enemy's room I dusted. The trip was a short one. I knocked on the door and stepped back. Guess who answered the door? I would never have guessed it, that was for damned sure. It was Group Captain Harhoff, the arbiter of my fight in the laundry. What were the odds of him being the one who just happened to need help because of an injured paw? Slim to none by my calculations. I had to be on my toes.

"Ah, Josbelub, thank you for accepting my offer. Please, come in," he said as he stood aside and swept his free arm to show me in.

"Not a problem. Fuffefer's a good boss. If he wants that I should help you, I'm all in."

"Excellent. Please, have a seat over there." Once I was down he said, "I'm a person of modest needs. I only ask that you keep the rooms clean. I will continue to use the laundry service and take my meals in the officers' mess, so you needn't worry about those tasks."

"Sounds like a working vacation to me."

"Yes, I suppose it will be."

He was being awful cheery and cordial. Very non-Adamant, in my experience.

"The layout of my quarters and Group-Single Fuffefer's are identical. All the supplies you might require will be in the same locations. Do you have any questions?"

"May I use your name to order some food for myself to be delivered here?"

"Of course. Whatever you fancy. Here, let me show you to your sleeping area and get you set up with some passcodes for the computers."

Over the next two days, I barely caught sight of Harhoff. He sure wasn't around enough to make any kind of mess. Pretty soon, I was just shining the dust that was still there from the day before. But I made a show of doing the old spit and polish. Before leaving to work the morning of my last day there, he shocked the hell out of me. He asked if I wouldn't mind preparing a meal for the two of us that evening to celebrate my outstanding service. What, was this a date? Did I need to bring condoms? I sure as hell hoped not.

By then, I knew what the canovir's palates were like, so I whipped up a dinner he'd enjoy. Why not? He'd been nice, if somewhat invisible to me. Just because I wished his entire species a violent death didn't mean I couldn't be the better man. So, I made braised liver—rare—boiled veggies—very not rare—and what looked to be rice. The entire apartment wreaked of liver. It reminded me of Sunday dinners at the grandparents, eons ago back on Earth, minus the onions.

Even before he stepped in, Harhoff took a deep whiff and

proclaimed, "It smells wonderful. Just like home." He, however, meant it in a positive manner, unlike me.

"Well, come on over and let's chow down."

He set what he was carrying down and went to a cupboard in the kitchen. He pulled out a bottle that, based on its markings, had to be something high proof. All right already.

He clinked two glasses down and pulled the stopper out of the bottle with his teeth.

"I hope you can drink musto. It's fermented and distilled fungil berries."

"Shouldn't be a problem, but we'll only know for sure after half a bottle or so."

"To the expansion of scientific knowledge." He raised his glass.

I did the same. "To science."

We belted back the firewater. Nice! After that, we served ourselves from the plates on the table between us. I may have been the hired help, but I wasn't inclined to serve him, and he didn't seem to care.

"Delicious," he said as he chewed the revolting, slimy liver. "Not overcooked. Perfect."

I put some in my mouth and turned my senses of taste and smell off. "Mmm. Just like Mom used to make."

"Really?" he asked with genuine interest.

"Unfortunately, yes."

"Ah, not a fan of liver?"

"Not so much."

"Well thank you for indulging me then."

"No problem. It was fun spending your money. This stuff's choice grade."

"I'm a bachelor. What's money for if not to spend it on the occasional indulgence?"

103

I rested my chin on the back of my hand. "Forgive me for saying it, but that doesn't sound very Adamant-like."

He thought a moment. "I guess it's not. We're not all identical, you know?"

"I hadn't noticed." I figured I'd push him a little to see what his game was. We'd also almost polished off the bottle of booze, so maybe his tongue was loosening up.

"Very funny. No, just as the five races differ, so do those amongst each race. Surely, it's the same where you come from. Ah, where was that?"

"Ungalaym." I felt that was a test.

"Yes, that's where Group-Single Fuffefer was stationed last, wasn't it?"

"Ah, I don't want trouble. If you want to know his service record, you'd better ask him." I toasted my last shot and threw it back.

"Yes, of course. Forgive me."

"Already forgotten. Seriously." I held up the glass. "Already gone."

"In that case, let me see if I have another bottle."

I started to explain what I meant, when it hit me. Why bother? The more booze the better.

He came back, displaying a little unsteadiness of gait. Note to self, it was more exaggerated than his stride leaving the room. He plopped into his chair and popped the top. He poured us each a full glass and rested back in his chair.

"What did you do back home?"

"I was a farmer. Most of my people are. It's good honest work."

He shuddered. "If you say so. It sounds like a prison sentence to me. No, I prefer the military life." He squinted at me. "You carry yourself like you are a military man, too. Am I right?"

I patted my chest. "Me? No way. I'm afraid of spiders and hate killing my own animals for food. No, I'm a certified pacifist."

"*Pacifist*, you say? I'll have to look that word up later." He chuckled softly. "You seemed to be handling Juyrot pretty handily."

"That little pup? If we were fighting, he wouldn't have been much of a match for anyone my size," I guffawed.

"I've been in combat with the fellow. He's more lethal than you might think. I've seen him kill enemies your size and bigger without difficulty. It would take an opponent of remarkable skill to best him. Remarkable."

"You said that twice."

"Because it would be *so* remarkable."

"I think you've had enough musto."

"Make a joke about it if you must, but what I say is true. In fact, I'd watch my back closely if I were you." He pointed a pinky claw at me.

"Like you told him, he doesn't want any part of Fuffefer. I'm not worried."

He stared at his glass a bit too long. "You hardly used the computer while you were here. Was there a problem with it?"

"No." I passed a finger over the remnants of the feast. "Witness the excess of overpriced foodstuffs purchased." Odd question. "There's not much else I might use the Adamant's computer system for. Your holovision is paralyzingly dull to me."

He snorted. "You and me *both*. Trash on a good day."

We raised our glasses to that.

"Well," I said, "it's getting late, and these dishes aren't going to do themselves." I began to stand.

"No, wait, Josbelub. I'll get them tomorrow. Sit."

"Your paw's all better?" I asked a bit too snarkily.

"It's fine now, thanks to you," he said without conviction. "Do you know why I was in the laundry that night when I broke up your fight?"

Uh-oh, this could be major trouble. "Ah, no. Honestly, I don't."

"I was on duty. I'm stationed on the bridge, you know. I'm responsible for computer and AI security."

"I did not know that." *Crap.* "Are you sure you should be discussing this with me?"

"No," he said, with a very serious look on his face. "In fact, I'm certain I shouldn't be. But I noticed some odd trafficking across the entire system that night."

"What I know about computers you could fit in Juyrot's left nostril *after* it swelled up."

That brought a chuckle.

"If you say so. I was able to trace the source of the input to the laundry area."

"How odd. I sure didn't see anything suspicious, not that I'd know what that was in the first place."

"I came down to investigate. Do you know what I saw?"

"No, but I'm thinking you're about to tell me."

"I saw the two of you brawling. That was a problem."

"How so? You told me you're not a Juyrot fan."

"No. If there was only one person there, he would be my likely suspect."

"But there were two, and they clearly weren't functioning as an effective espionage team."

"*Clearly* not."

"So, why not arrest us both, torture us for the information, or what the heck, just toss us both out the nearest external hatch?"

"Why not, indeed?"

I sipped some musto and stared at him. *Wait.* "If you were

simply trying to protect the ship's systems, that is *precisely* what you'd have done. And you wouldn't have wandered into a computer break-in alone. You'd have half the soldiers on duty in front of you. You wanted to know *who* was being naughty because there exist some reasons to be naughty that you'd be inclined to favor. If, for example, you were not as fully committed to the emperor's long-term plans, you might kind of wonder if there was another like-minded soul in the laundry area."

I tapped my forehead with the back of a finger. "But there's a gap in that line of reasoning."

"Do tell."

"There were only two possible candidates, Juyrot and me. If he was as loyal as he is rock-stupid, you couldn't mention the hacking. So, you can't trust him unless he was the only one down there and the culprit. He'd sound an alarm otherwise."

"Where's the gap you spoke of?"

"If he's loyal, he wouldn't be breaking into the computer. But that would mean it had to have been *me*. If you knew that, you'd be safe to just up and ask me."

"Very good. But there exists a possibility you can't know about. There are *factions* amongst the Adamant. Some are more warlike and aggressive than the group that currently holds power. Some others favor alternate leadership, so to speak."

I raised my hand. "So Juyrot *could* have been working for a terrorist cell. That would make him a candidate for the sabotage, too. It would make him a more dangerous candidate. Your run-of-the-mill alien spy might be a nuisance, but a subversive agent would have to be silenced fast."

"So, a cautious individual would spend a few days vetting the possible subversive while —"

"At the same time observing the possible alien spy," I

snapped, finishing his thought. "And I'm guessing you came to the decision that dumb-as-a-flagpole Juyrot didn't do anything to suggest he was bright enough to be a covert operative."

"He most certainly did not. There was nothing in his files to support such capabilities either."

"Hence, you concluded I was the hacker, which, of course, I'm not. If you came to that incorrect opinion, and you were a big old fan of Bestiormax, you'd have put a plasma bolt in the back of my head by now. In fact, if you were a player in any faction opposing the boss, you'd have done the same thing. That leaves only one real possibility. You're against *all* the war-loving Adamant. You are, in fact, a pacifist and will not need to look the word up."

He clapped his paws and smiled broadly. "Very good reasoning for a farmer."

"Since I'm a simple country boy, I'm guessing here, but let me ask you something. *If* you were a pacifist subversive and anyone in any other faction knew it, you'd be so dead it would be ugly, right?"

He nodded gently.

"So, isn't telling me kind of putting your life in my hands? Which, I might add, would be ludicrously suicidal, since I'd be crazy not to tell my master, if he was, in fact, my master?"

"Yes, *Jon Ryan*, that would be the case."

I leaned my chair back onto two legs and smiled like the cat that ate all the canaries. "I love it when I'm right."

TWENTY

"Seriously, Slapgren, she was insane. I'm really scared." Mirraya was trembling.

"Relax," he responded confidently. "She hated our guts before. How can that get worse? You know I'm right."

"This is different. She was mean, heartless, and cruel before. Now she's lost her mind. She's determined to make all of us suffer more than anyone has suffered before. I know she means it."

"Hang on a sec. Who's all of us? I just count two." He pointed to her. "One." He pointed to himself. "Two."

Mirri cracked half a smile. "There's another part I haven't told you about yet. Um, she is going to supervise a new program when she's better."

"What kind of program? I'm not liking the sound of it."

"Well, ya just might. She's going to force breed us."

"Force feed us. Whatever for? I eat all the time as it is."

"No. Force *breed* us. You know, have us make babies. And then she'll torture them, too."

"Ah, the first part doesn't sound all that bad. The second part, wow. It really sucks."

"The first part really sucks, too. *You're* still a child. And I refuse to be mated like a prize *rostalop*."

"Is she planning on making this an optional activity?"

"Hardly," Mirri said with disgust.

"Then your objection or mine doesn't matter much."

"Not if we escape or kill her or Uncle Jon finally gets here."

"Unlikely, less likely, and least likely."

"I have to stay positive."

"And about you calling me a child. I'd really appreciate it if you stopped that. I'm a young adult."

"Slappy, we're not talking what grade you are in school, but whether you're *metabolically* an adult."

"I am, too."

She leaned against a bare wall. "So, are you going to tell me you're sexually mature? I don't recall hearing of Mrs. Slapgren or Slapgrenettes."

"I don't have kids, but I know I'm ready." He scuffed the floor with his heel. "I've been sort of practicing a little, you know, and it works."

"Can my day get any worse? A madwoman threatens me with endless torture, and now I have to deal with the image of you playing with yourself. Where's a stick to gouge out my eyes?"

"Hey, it not that unusual. And I wouldn't call it *playing* with myself. I'm practicing for adulthood."

"When you're an adult, you don't need to jerk yourself off. You'll have a mate who's stuck with that unenviable task." She flicked a finger against his forehead. "Disgusting child." She pointed at him intently. "And if I ever catch you doing it, so help me, I'll make you regret it, hopefully involving permanent psychological scars."

Sentorip rushed into the room. She had her satchel of medical supplies. "Mastress," she said breathlessly, "I heard you were taken to see that awful Adamant as soon as she could think straight. Where are you hurt?" She was forcing Mirri into a chair while inspecting her meticulously.

"I'm fine, sweet Sentorip. Yes, she's alive, but she's very weak. Didn't even have the strength to pull a hair from my head."

Sentorip smiled faintly. "So, it went well? How surprising."

"Hardly. She threatened us with the worst torture and torment any living soul has ever endured. She said she'll force us to mate so she can inflict even more suffering on our children." Mirraya slipped unconsciously into Sentorip's arms, and hugged her powerfully. "It was awful, Sentorip. I know she means it and can do it.

"But what was I to do? I was presented with my one and only chance to strike at her. I had to. Curse me for my weakness. I shouldn't have tried if I knew there was a chance of not finishing her."

"You would have, my friend, but for her guards. You couldn't fight their plasma rifles *and* finish off Malraff. It was not your fault."

There was a sound coming from the hallway. A handful of footsteps approached. Sentorip focused on the open door, waiting to see who was coming. Doctor Pastersal entered the room, head down, reading a handheld. Three soldiers accompanied him.

When the doctor was a couple meters away, Sentorip pushed off Mirraya's chest and jumped backward with all her might. She crashed into a table, smashing it. She scampered to her feet and assumed a four-legged defensive posture. "How dare you insult the glorious emperor by insulting his gift of a Descore. I can handle your constant insults, but *physically* I'm no match for your blows." She held up a bent wrist. "I think you broke it this time, bitch." Sentorip cradled the injured appendage.

"What's going on here?" demanded the doctor.

"She kicked me in my belly. She said I smelled as bad as the food I prepared for her and then she kicked me again."

"Is that what happened?" he said to Mirri.

"I...I don't know what happened. One moment we were talking and the next she's airborne."

"You kicked me and you know it," growled Sentorip. "You can't lie to an Adamant. They don't care if you beat us to death. But they will not tolerate lying. Go ahead, tell him how you've been beating me viciously since the day we met."

"B ... but Sentorip, you know that's not true. You're my friend."

Sentorip pointed to the doctor as a witness. "See how she mocks me, too? Addressing me by my first name and making me the laughingstock by calling me her friend in public. It is more than I can bear."

"You hate this Descore so much that you would abuse her? She was a gift from His Imperial Emperor. Are there words you can say to justify such reprehensible behavior?" challenged the doctor.

"No. It's all a misunderstanding. I would never..."

"Hold your tongue, alien, before you commit further crimes. I will deal with you later. First, I must attend to the injured wrist you have caused." Turning to Sentorip, he said, "These males will escort you to sick bay. I will see you there momentarily."

Sentorip left with the guards. Looking over her shoulder at Mirraya, she winked.

"There will be consequences, dirt-eating child," growled Pastersal. "First you nearly kill the high seer, now you maim an innocent servant. You should be put down." With that, he turned his back and stormed out of the room.

Slapgren and Mirri stood alone on the cell. No one bothered to return Slapgren to his own cell, as was protocol.

"Wow, that went weird," said Slapgren. "Ah, why'd you hit your friend?"

"I didn't, you nitwit."

"Huh?"

"Didn't you see her wink at me?"

"Wink at you? Are you crazy? I didn't see it, but even if I did, what does that mean?"

"A few weeks back she and I were talking, just idle chatter to pass the time. She asked me what I missed most about Uncle Jon. I told her I missed his winks."

"Uncle Jon winks?"

In a huff, she shot back, "Yes, he most certainly *does*."

"Never saw him wink, I don't think." He rubbed the side of his head. "What's the big deal about him winking? Maybe he just has a nervous tick. My grandfather had one. Man, was it annoying. He'd —" He trailed off when he noticed Mirri's harsh stare and folded arms.

"Uncle Jon winks to be cute. When he does something silly or infuriating, he winks."

"So Sentorip wanted to say she was being silly?"

"No, child. She was doing it to reassure me, the same way Uncle Jon always does."

"I thought you said..."

"You only hear my words, not my meaning. You're such a boy."

"Huh? I..."

"She's up to something. I just wish I knew what so I could help her."

"Mirri, you know she's the kindest, gentlest soul alive. But I don't think she's capable of formulating, let alone executing, a complex scheme."

"I think we're going to find out if that's true or not."

TWENTY-ONE

"So, when did you figure out who I really was?" I asked Harhoff as he sipped his musto.

"Only just recently. You've been big news on all Adamant channels for a while, but we knew little about you. Then you pulled that brave, stupid stunt on *Excess of Nothing*. Since then not only do we know what you look like, you've risen to be obsession number one of the Adamant leaders. The emperor asks for hourly updates on whether you're dead yet. Your picture appears on all computer screens in the right upper corner. That's where Bestiormax's face used to be until he decided that catching you was more important than honoring his ego."

"Hmm," I said, swirling my musto as I stared through it, "that would make anyone ratting me out pretty important. The rewards would be phenomenal."

"Indeed, they are. But you're worth much more to me than promotions and money."

"I'm that cute?"

"Hardly." He giggled. "You're not my type by sex and species both. Personally, I find you revolting."

I raised my glass. "Here's to revolting." I belted it back. "Let's keep it that way."

He raised his glass to that and pounded it down. "Ehhh," he said because of the burn, "that's good stuff."

"So why, my new friend, am I so very valuable?"

He set his glass down and leaned forward. "I'll assume you don't know much about our history."

"That would be a safe assumption. I just know a lot about your current propensities."

He rested back and looked thoughtful. "Our origins are obscure even to ourselves. Suffice it to say, we've been around a very long time. The historical records are excellent for at least a billion years. In that time, we've grown larger, smarter, and more aggressive."

"Not a sociable trend."

"Hardly. As we grew in those qualities, so did our appetite to control. We strove for greater control of ourselves, others, the physical world—everything. And we did so well. For hundreds of millions of years, we've conquered, subjugated, and organized. There are more canovir now than even *we* can count. We are in more places than we are actually aware of, we're so massive. And we are *still* expanding exponentially. I think we now rule the local group of galaxies. That's fifty or so entire mega systems."

"Don't get too self-impressed. Most of those are *dwarf* galaxies."

"Make light of it, if you will. My point is this. Our incomprehensibly mammoth society is controlled by one individual, the emperor." He held up one claw. "Imagine that. *One* person rules and runs it all. There's been nothing like that in the history of the known universe."

"All very fascinating, I'm sure, but can we get back to what makes me so valuable amidst all this dog glory?"

"In all that volume of control, in all that span of time, you alone, Jon Ryan of Earth, have done more damage to us than any other foreign agent. You have resisted the irresistible, defeated the indomitable, and frustrated the unstoppable. That makes you more valuable than all the wealth the emperor hordes."

"That's an eloquent speech, and my ego thanks you profusely, but just because I get a little lucky, how does that make me valuable beyond the dreams of avarice?"

"I assure you luck has nothing to do with what you've accomplished. Someone must win all lotteries. If luck, random chance alone could lead to our losing one battle, some race somewhere must have done it before. No, your achievements are unique and are based on you."

"I'm still looking for why that's valuable?'

"Surely the great Jon Ryan can see the value in that ability?"

"Of course, I can. What I asked was what makes me valuable to *you*, Group Captain Harhoff, pacifist."

He lowered his head a second. "You know better than anyone what becomes of all dominant species."

"They falter, fade, and are forgotten. Sure."

"And so it must be eventually with us."

"And?"

"And once the inevitable happens, what will follow?"

"Chaos, deprivation, mass extinctions, and no reliable Wi-Fi service."

"I would wish that not to be our legacy. I would wish for a kinder, gentler passing into a better future."

"Okay, so you're in line to receive a bunch of humanitarian awards. Where do I fit in?"

"As the sole agent, the only individual to successfully resist our tidal wave, you are a rallying point. You..."

"Oh no," I cut him off sharply. "I can see where that locomotive is heading, and the answer is *no*. My second answer, after long reflection and soul-searching, is *hell* no. My final answer, after being locked away in solitude for a century, is no *fucking* way."

"You did not hear me out."

"And I won't. What I'll be doing is thanking you for the booze, polishing off the last of said booze, and then retreating to my cushy position as Fuffefer's Descore." I stood, knocked back the contents of my glass, and turned to the door.

Over my shoulder I heard, "The great Jon Ryan doesn't need a cushy job wiping some asshole's butt. No, the great Jon Ryan is wiping said asshole's butt for a higher reason. I'm certain a laudable reason."

I keyed the door open.

"Only the formidable spy must not be able to achieve his lofty goal as it currently stands. But if he had help, say the help of a highly placed officer with an unimpeachable record of service, he might be able to achieve his aim."

I keyed the door shut.

"It seems the great Jon Ryan is able to listen to reason. None of us, my new friend, are islands."

TWENTY-TWO

"Does this hurt?" asked Doctor Pastersal as he pressed on Sentorip's joint.

She winced. "Just a little. Your holding it helps," she said, bashfully looking away.

Pastersal released her leg like it was hot. "It appears to be just a sprain, but I'll get an image just to be certain."

"That is so *kind* of you, Doctor. You are a good person to extend your wisdom to a Descore."

He fidgeted nervously. "Nonsense. My role is to care for all canovir regardless of race. Come, set your arm over here."

She rested her arm on a metal plate for a split second.

Pastersal went to a screen and tapped some keys. "Ah, no problem. Your arm is fine. Please, you may return to your seat over there." He pointed to the exam table. "My assistant will be in shortly to splint the arm, and then you're free to go." He turned to leave.

"Doctor Pastersal, might this lowly Descore ask a favor of someone so mighty?"

He stepped back to her, but remained a bit farther away than before. "Yes, you may."

"Well, I actually have a medical question, and I wish to be so bold as to ask for your assistance in a personal matter."

He shifted nervously. "I'll see what I can do. Ask your question."

"Since I've been in the service of the vile alien bitch, I have stopped cycling. You know, I haven't gone into heat. I used to be more regular than clockwork. Normally it would be no great matter, but I was told I would be allowed to have a litter with my next cycle. I so looked forward to it, but I am now so disappointed."

"I..."

"Not that it matters much anyway. As a Descore, I would likely only be able to attract another of my race, or possibly a Warrior if I were lucky." She blinked. "I'd never attract an Adamant such as yourself." She shot her elbow in front of her muzzle. "I can't *believe* I just said that. Please forgive me. Do not think poorly of me for such silly words." She turned her covered face away.

"Ah, no ... no need to apologize. I'm ... it's only natural, I'm told. Anyway, you are not cycling because of a device we're using to stop the aliens from shape-shifting. You can understand. Witness the unprovoked vicious attack your Mastress inflicted on the high seer when that device was disabled."

"Is the effect harmful?" she asked with a gasp. "I won't be permanently affected, will I?"

"I doubt it. Frankly we've not much experience with the device. It affects us all, so we try to avoid contact where possible."

"And if you turn it off, I can cycle and have my litter?"

"It's not my place to say. The security of the crew is the

most important factor."

"That leads me to the favor I might ask. In fact, it strengthens my desire for your aid. I will always do what I am told to do, know that. However, I wish to not suffer under that horrid alien's pernicious temper and foul disposition any longer. I also know the poor high seer has sustained grievous injuries and has barely escaped death. I would ask to be transferred into her service."

"Again, it is not mine to..."

"Oh, but it is. You see, this would be a great *medical* benefit to the high seer. I could assist you in bringing her back to her former excellent condition. The things a trained Descore can bring to the bowl are formidable, I assure you."

"You raise a valid point. She's extremely headstrong. I can ask her..."

"But she's not the physician, and she's not even currently mentally balanced. Surely you can insist. If it were your wise decision, surely she'd accept my humble aid." She looked to the floor. "Plus, if I am away from that wretched device and cycle, you would be close at paw to provide input. This being my first attempt at breeding, at being with a male in that way, the input of a skilled physician would be invaluable."

He stared at her open mouthed for a few seconds. "Your thoughts are valid. I'll see what I can do." He turned to leave, then whipped back to her. "No. I will not see. I will order it. Consider it done. You will work with the ailing high seer and I will be here to, er, help you should you ... *when* you come into heat."

"Thank you so much, good doctor. I could only dream of whelping a litter of pups as noble and wise as you. A girl can dream, can't she?"

He raised a paw to speak but dropped it to his side. He left without further comment.

TWENTY-THREE

"I'm sitting back down and listening to your proposals, Harhoff. I have three conditions. One, I want to know exactly what you can do to help me rescue the Deft kids. They are who I was trying to free on *Excess of Nothing*. Two, if I'm going to be the iconic rallying point that you desire more than wealth or power, I want to know *precisely* what you expect of me. Three," I held up the empty bottle of musto, "you'll need to produce about three more of these before we begin."

Harhoff angled his head and gave a throaty whine. "That third one may be the hardest. I'm afraid musto is hard to come by. My betters consider intoxicants unacceptable. They dull the mind and one's ability to serve the empire."

I made a show of folding my arms and looking resolute.

He left the room and returned with one bottle. "This is honestly all I have. I was saving it for a special occasion—one that involves a bitch, not another male." He bit the cork and spat it to the floor. Gazing at the bottle, he said, "Alas, my native wit and charm will have to suffice when the opportunity presents itself." He poured two full glasses.

"I'll give you lessons, and you'll be fine."

"I doubt your techniques and insights would work with Adamant females."

"My style works on *all* the ladies," I scoffed back. I took a big swig of musto.

"As to your first condition, I don't know really."

"How very unencouraging and non-inspirational. You really should avoid careers in politics or door-to-door sales, my friend."

"I'm not saying I can't be very helpful, only that I don't know how specifically. We need to discuss at length what you know and what costs you are willing to pay."

"Do you have allies—like-minded Adamant—who can help?"

"Yes and no."

"Again, less than reassuring. Do you guys have life coaches you can consult?"

"I mean to say I know a few and they know a few. Our points of view are most lethal if exposed."

"So, you have small cells. The cell members only know each other. Only one of you need know someone higher up in the chain, to prevent the total collapse of the subversives if anyone is captured."

"Basically. You are familiar with such a structure?"

"Yeah. Pretty basic clandestine operating procedure. So, all in all, how many freethinkers like you are there?"

"Obviously, I don't know. I'd estimate maybe half a percent of the Adamant. So, there are a lot, but we are massively outnumbered."

"Hmm. Interesting. Are there pacifists in the highest ranks? How about the emperor's inner circle?"

"That I do not know. I'm only a mid-level individual. High-ranking subversives, sure, there must be some. As to the emperor's court, it would be less likely. His contacts are closely vetted and monitored."

"Are you guys willing to die for your cause?" I fixed my attention on his eyes.

"Yes," he replied without hesitation. "We all understand what's at stake, both in terms of risks and benefits."

"That's something. What about what you expect of me?"

"There I can be more specific."

"I figured as much."

"Currently the Adamant are spread across all the stars in the sky. Our numbers and power have grown exponentially for as long as anyone can remember. Titular power rests with the emperor, but, trust me, he's much more interested in his next illicit piece of tail, not his abundant empire. The actual iron control comes from the military leadership that accompanies him. Even if he tried to take control and order some action, they'd ignore his order while reporting back it was a spectacular success."

"Wait, they deceive him, everybody knows it, and it still goes on without heads flying every which way?"

"Yes. He's so preoccupied with his personal goals, he has no problem turning a blind eye or two."

"Okay, he's a narcissistic loser, but what about all those gazillions of emperors before him?"

"They're cut from the same indulgent cloth. Oh, on rare occasions an emperor will step out of the shadows and try to assume control."

"It doesn't sound like he's allowed to."

"No. That rare breed is subject to bizarre accidents or remarkably premature health issues."

"So how do I fit into your plans?"

"The entire military focuses on the Secure Council. Those

are the players who actually call the shots. There are twelve of them. Their terms last until they die."

"Of natural causes or others."

"Those are the rules. With all eyes and ears trained on them, order and discipline are maintained. Their words are final and their orders are carried out. That is how it has always been. But, if their master vision was undercut sufficiently, their monolith of power would crumble quickly."

"Why do you think that? I mean, they're good at using fear and might to get what they want. A few losses wouldn't change that."

"My group is betting it will. Remember, the Adamant are spread so thinly and so far that even we don't know the extent of our empire. Out there," he pointed to the ceiling, "there are millions of commanders itching to take control. They know their chance of being a member of the Secure Council is zero. If they have risen to a lofty position and they're not close to such a dream, then it is impossible by sheer numbers and the vast distances involved.

"You know well, General Ryan, the undeniable desires that live in powerful leaders' hearts. They all want more. Due to the ruthlessness and the hypervigilant nature of our military structure, they can never achieve the only thing they truly want. But if there were a disruption of that iron-fisted control, I'm betting tens of thousands of wannabe kings would fall all over each other to assume local control. If such a process begins, it can never be stopped."

"You can't put the genie back in the bottle."

"I'm at a disadvantage here. What's a genie, and what bottle do they come in?"

"Old human legend. A genie is a magical spirit trapped in a bottle. If you free it, it becomes your slave and you rule the world."

He wrinkled his brow. "If it's that powerful, why doesn't it let itself out of the bottle?"

"It's legend, a fairy tale. They're not supposed to make sense."

"Then why do they exist?"

"You guys don't have fanciful stories that double as object lessons that you tell your pups at night?"

"No. Why would we? If we wish a lesson taught, we teach it. In no way does fiction advance the goals of a stable, cohesive, productive society."

"If you say so. If I gum all this up to the tiny extent I might be able to if very lucky, you think that would bring the entire house of cards tumbling down?"

"That depends on your definition of tiny."

"This isn't sounding good. Let me turn the question around. What's your idea of tiny?"

He held up a single claw. "The catastrophic destruction of one single ship."

"Did I tell you I'm a prophet?"

He jerked his head back in surprise. "You are a what?"

"Yeah, a pretty good one. Here, I'll write three words down on this napkin. Then you tell me which single, tiny ship I'd need to make go boom boom." I handed him the slip.

He opened it and smiled. "Why, it appears you are gifted. Yes, you only have to destroy the emperor's ship, ideally with both him and the Secure Council aboard."

"And if they're not?"

"The initial reports, I guarantee you, will state that they were."

"So, you think eliminating the central control will spiral the entire empire into disarray and disorder?"

"I'm betting my life it will."

"And if it doesn't?"

"It won't concern either of us what transpires if it does not."

"Sales. That's another career path you should avoid. You really stink at it."

TWENTY-FOUR

"I asked Darfey, and he says he doesn't know. Either that or he's too frightened to tell me," Slapgren said, trying to sound reassuring.

"But she's been gone for three days. I'm beginning to think she's not coming back," replied Mirri as she wrung her hands.

"Whether she does or doesn't isn't something you have any control over."

"But I'm certain she was trying to tell me she had a plan."

"Then she has a plan."

"Don't be soft-headed," she scolded. "She's a great servant and a sweetheart, but becoming a covert operative is nothing she could pull off. If she tried, I'm afraid they'll expose her immediately and ... and then she'll be gone."

"If that's what happened, that's what happened. Again, what are we supposed to do about it?"

"We could mourn her, for one."

"Here's a good compromise. You mourn her, and I'll focus on the fact that we're..."

"What? Why'd you stop in the middle of speaking, stupid?"

"Did you feel that?"

"Obviously not. What didn't I feel?"

He held up his hand. His forearm melted and reshaped as a scaled club.

"Oh my," she squeaked. Mirri melted and became a Horta, hissing on the floor. Then, as quickly as possible, she went back to herself. "Reform *now*. We need to concentrate. *Crap*, we should have planned for this before."

"What?"

"What can we become for short periods that can help us after we return to Deft form?"

"You mean dig holes to escape out of?"

"Yeah, maybe. No. I don't know. Something useful."

"I could become a saber-toothed backwallow and you could rip a fang out. We could —"

"You'd eat me with the other three out of instinct."

"Sorry."

"Wait." She flopped on her belly and melted. She reformed into a bulbous lizard-like tube with fifty tiny pairs of legs. The front pair, however, were massively enlarged—basically lobster claws that terminated at the rubbery mouth. The olifar spit out a pair of fleshy balls and quickly spit out two more. Then Mirri turned back into herself.

As she rearranged her disrupted robes, Slapgren asked, "What the heck was that?"

She returned him a dubious glance. "An olifar. You're telling me *you*, a boy, don't know what they are?"

He shrugged. "What?"

She pointed to the balls. "It produces pouches of a powerful toxin and then uses those front claws to throw them at threats."

"How *cool*. Can I become one, too?"

"We'll see. Here, hide these two, but be careful. If they rupture you might die."

"Totally cool. I'm all over this," he said as he went into the next room to stash them.

When they regrouped, she said, "We can't know why that happened or how long it will last. We need to think very hard for other assets we can produce when it happens again."

"Yeah, too bad we can't turn into a plasma rifle factory."

"Right. Yeah, too bad. Do try and think of something we can become, okay?"

"This'll be fun. I can think of a few *nasty* things already."

"Remember, we have to become something that will produce a weapon *after* we change back, and we have to return to normal fast. If we're locked in an alien form, they'll know we're up to something. You got that?"

He looked at her like she was clueless. "Of course, I do. I'm *not* stupid."

She smiled back. "Oh, and keep pressing your Descore on what happened to Sentorip."

"I will. *Geez*, you treat me like I'm a kid," he scoffed.

Again, she just smiled back.

TWENTY-FIVE

Harhoff and I talked for several hours that first meeting, solving all the problems in the universe, it would seem. He really didn't have any more musto, which was a pity. The stuff went down well. He reassured me there were many things he could do to help me achieve retaking *Stingray* and destroying *Excess of Nothing*. Neither, he conceded, would be easy. Basically, he asked me to come up with a few contingencies and run them by him. That way he could figure out how he and his cell could help. Importantly, he didn't place any time pressure on me. If he had, I'd have been suspicious. Hell, the Adamant empire had been running wild across space for billions of years. There needn't be a rush to initiate their slow demise.

I raised the ever-looming issue of Evil Jon. He knew there were two of us from reports coming off Azsuram. He wasn't sure he bought the whole alternate time line story, but that really didn't matter. He understood the dude was trouble with a capital T, which was the essential takeaway point. I let him know the issues with EJ. He'd defeated me once and probably could again unless something fundamental changed. He also wanted my teens. Protecting them, not ending a cruel empire, was my number-one priority. He thought that was silly but accepted the reality.

He sketched a picture of Adamant security procedures. Man, were they tight—much more draconian than I'd imagined. Everybody watched and reported on everybody else. Also, there were three separate security agencies whose sole purpose was to watch the other two and everybody else while they were at it. The bottom line was that we'd have to be more than extremely careful in contacting one another or we'd be caught faster than fish in a barrel. Harhoff thought my cover as Descore to Fuffefer was fine for the time being. It turned out my benefactor was a hound of great status and outstanding breeding. His rank as Group-Single was remarkable because he was still very young. There were rumors the emperor had an eye on him. That made him a safe wall to hide behind.

Because I was a skeptical guy, I didn't let Harhoff know about *Whoop Ass* trailing us at a distance. I wanted my ace-in-the-hole card to remain my secret. There were too many suspicious elements at play for me to get overconfident. I was periodically in contact with GB and was certain that he was still undetected.

Harhoff and I set a signal we could use to indicate when either of us wanted to communicate with the other. I suggested a radio link like GB and I had, but he felt that would be too risky. Again, I left off telling him I hadn't had any trouble sneaking messages off the ship.

That next morning, I returned to my post with Fuffefer. Though he was a tight-ass like me, I could tell he was happy to have me back. Either he missed the convenience I provided or the son of a bitch actually missed *me*. Naturally, I favored the latter explanation.

132

"So, the Group Captain wasn't too tough on you?" he asked jokingly, which was totally out of character for him.

"Naw. The beatings were infrequent, and he's not nearly as strong as he looks. He whips like a puppy."

That brought a genuine laugh.

"When I need to beat you, I'll keep in mind that you kiss and tell." He flexed an arm muscle. "I'd best hit the gym to bulk up."

Nice guy. I was beginning to like him. That was dangerous. He was everything I hated in my new existence, and he was my sworn enemy. Life, I concluded, and not for the first time, was funny and full of unanticipated turns and wiggles. I had to remind myself that if it came to it, I'd snap him like a dry twig.

"Any update on my many detractors and haters?" I asked.

"No. That's good, by the way. The longer you're here, the less likely it is that the captain will insist on your removal."

"*Removal.* That sounds different than *fired*, taken as a word all by itself. I'm wondering if *removal* hurts more than plain old *fired*."

"You are too clever for your own good, Josbelub Pontared. Around me, that is fine. I suggest you keep a blanket over it in public, all right?"

"I value your praise *and* your counsel."

He shook his head disapprovingly. That was a familiar sight in my long life. I considered it a good thing. We wiseasses had reputations to enhance and protect.

We settled back into our bone-achingly dull routine soon enough. I did a little cleaning and stocking, and he tried to ignore me but found it increasingly difficult. Normally an Adamant spoke to a Descore only as a god to his worshipper. Old Fuff was coming to enjoy the luxury of private conversations with a non-threatening listener. The Adamant society was so damn suspicious and political that any unfiltered thoughts were likely to be one's last. I had to admit that the insights he provided me into their culture were fascinating, even when they weren't specifically useful militarily. Their historical tales were unbelievable.

There was a time, it was rumored but never recorded, that the Adamant weren't so dominant. He told me it had to be many millions of years ago, but there was a time when his race lived as traders and even farmers. He claimed they excelled at both, which I totally believed. When the Adamant set their minds to something, they did it better than anyone else. He said that in those days, the five races mixed seamlessly and functioned as one balanced society. He made it sound like he approved of the normalcy of a cohesive, goal-sharing culture. This was an example of a thought he didn't dare share with another Adamant. To suggest that they weren't the apex of creation was a foolish thought. Foolish thoughts came from foolish Adamant. Foolish Adamant did not exist. End of story.

After a couple weeks back at my post with Fuffefer, I decided to risk hacking the computer system again. Harhoff had told me how he detected my intrusion and gave me suggestions how to better infiltrate the system. He couldn't supply me with passwords because they could easily be traced back to him.

I was glad for his help. Since my last visit, I learned there had been trouble on *Dare Not*. I found a reference to a report filed by a Doctor Pastersal to the Secure Council that High Seer Malraff was "assaulted and seriously injured but expected to live." There were no details. His odd choice of words struck me. Assaulted and seriously injured but expected to live. Who attacked a high seer, whatever that was, on her own ship? Rodents of unusual size from the bowels of the ship? Not hardly. Crew members could have. But my research suggested *Dare Not* was her ship, her *home*. I'd met the bitch. She'd leave zero to chance. She'd have to, because she was so darn mean. All crew members would be loyal beyond question.

That the good doctor only *expected* her to live was curious. He hadn't said "we're fighting like hell to keep her alive" or "her condition is so grave she's to be transferred to a better care team." No. I kind of pictured him yawning and declaring that he *expected* her to survive. It didn't surprise me that no one mourned the freakazoid's misfortune, because no one in or out of their right mind could possibly *like* Malraff. But the lack of, I don't know, dedication or passion to her recovery seemed out of character for these guys.

I did know Malraff was the one holding the gun to Mirraya's head, so they were together at that point in time. If she'd taken my kids with her when she returned to *Dare Not*, it sure put a smile on my face to think it was one of the teens who'd assaulted her. Those kids could be nasty-plus if given the chance. Their ability to shape-shift was suppressed, but all systems failed. It could be one of them was responsible for ripping Malraff a bunch of new holes.

Why would a high seer take the last two Deft to her home base? A nurturing and family atmosphere were unlikely explanations. I determined I had to find out what a high seer did, what it was they were supposed to see. But asking questions in Adamant society was risky business. If I asked Fuffefer what seers did, he'd have to wonder why I wanted to know. As far as I knew, there weren't any aboard *Rush to Glory* for me to be curious about. The topic was too important to let drop, so I signaled Harhoff that I wanted to meet. He might light into me for doing so for this reason, but I had no choice.

We met in the mess. I had established a pattern of eating there occasionally specifically so it wouldn't be unusual for me to be there when Harhoff also happened to be there. He sat in the table right smack dab in the middle of the room, and I chanced to notice him. He graciously invited me to join him. He didn't have to ask the officers dining with him to leave. They bolted like I was a polecat with leaky glands. For a while, we made empty chatter designed to lose the interest of any one eavesdropping nearby. We did a good job. I was bored out of my gourd. I started playing *Candy Crush* while talking. I'd gotten addicted to it on my initial space flight back on *Ark 1*. Call me juvenile, but I was really bored.

Finally, Harhoff felt it was safe. "What's up?" he asked in a conversational tone. He didn't want to attract attention by dropping his volume.

"I need to know what a high seer is," I said to my soup.

"*Hah*. Seriously?" He laughed like I'd told a funny joke. "You risk our lives to discover something you could look up in a dictionary? Well, my fault, I didn't say you couldn't contact me for help with crossword puzzles, did I?"

"I need to know what they really do, not what their official job description says. Specifically, I want to know about High Seer Malraff. Do you know her?"

"Fortunately, I do not. Few do, and almost all of them disappear soon after they meet the bitch."

"So, you know her by reputation?"

"Colorful and frightful would be the words I'd choose. That and sociopath."

"I had the same impression when I met her."

"You've survived the pleasure of meeting the Storm From Hell?"

"That her nickname?"

"And a well-earned one." He set down his utensil and folded his front paws thoughtfully. "I had a friend a few years back. He was a good officer and talented. He was more dedicated than most Adamant, which is saying a lot. He was also more devoted to our current, dubiously talented emperor. He was like a puppy to him, he was so devoted.

"He transferred away to a new ship. It was a small promotion, but he glowed in the dark, he was so pleased. We kept in touch. He was promoted once again to a position most Adamant would consider a dead-end insult of an assignment, but not Rathwor. No, every move up was a place he could better serve his beloved emperor."

"Somehow, I think there's a cautionary end to this tale," I said darkly.

"Indeed. My friend was as socially inept as he was militarily skilled. While meeting his new shipmates, it became clear to them he was a two-legged rabbit at bentil. That's a popular card game amongst the military."

"You mean he was an easy mark at poker?"

"Your idiom sounds right. So naturally he was enticed into every crooked game aboard ship. I tried to warn him, but he insisted Adamant would never cheat at cards and were only inviting him to be sociable. Then, one day, the impossible happened."

"The two-legged rabbit won it all. He took everybody's ill-gotten gains."

"Yes, he did. As a total newbie, completely unaware of his tenuous position, he boasted of it to everyone he could. Well, one of the individuals who lost a fortune that night was the son of a member of the Secret Council."

"That doesn't sound healthy."

"It very much isn't. So, the sore loser cries to Papa that he was cheated out of honest money and that the thief was belittling the family name."

I whistled.

"Two days later, *Dare Not* docks with Rathwor's ship. He's

137

summoned from sleep to the captain's cabin, where he is introduced to Malraff. Captain said there had been charges he'd cheated at cards. Even as Rathwor babbled of his innocence, Malraff said she'd been sent by the Secure Council to investigate the charges. She told him cheating at bentil was a high crime. It undermined the integrity of the fighting forces that relied on the game as a pleasant respite from the serious duties of advancing the empire.

"Rathwor was still incoherently shouting that he was innocent as he disappeared onto *Dare Not*. He was never heard from or seen again."

"Ouch."

"Tell me about it. I was even foolish enough to contact his family a good while later. I figured he was dead, but I was damn curious. Anyway, he'd given me his family information in case he was killed so I could personally contact them. You'll never guess what his mother said when she heard my inquiry."

He stared at me a moment. "She said she never had a son. She had two daughters, but neither were in the military. Then she ended the transmission. The woman I was talking to was the same woman whose portrait hung in Rathwor's cabin. Within twenty minutes, the number was disconnected. In an even stupider stunt, once I was head of cybersecurity on this ship, I searched for Rathwor's military file."

"And, big surprise, there was none."

"Loyal, harmless Rathwor had been erased because he made a Secure Council member's card-cheating son look bad. They took all his money, too."

"So, all high seers are mindless killers? They're the goon squad?"

"They are a unique subset of the Adamant. If we had a religion, they might be considered our ministers."

"Are there priests?"

"No. The Loserandi are—were—the priests. They're all dead because they challenged the Adamant long ago. No, though seers are *not* priests, they're *quite similar* to them."

"Lunatic fringe with a personal agenda that suits the emperor's needs."

"Yes, that's fair to say. And Malraff is the worst I've ever heard of."

"Would it be fair to say all high seers act like her?"

He thought a second. "No. Most are heavy-handed, to be certain, but they're not cold-blooded killers. They police the Adamant from a purity of thought angle, I suppose you could say." He sipped his tea. "You say Malraff was with your Deft teens on *Excess of Nothing*? Do you know why?"

"Never got the chance to ask. She acted like she was in charge though."

He angled his head. "No, they don't command by rank. Fear, most definitely, but never directly."

"I think she took them to *Dare Not* with her."

He took a deep breath. "Then I doubt they'll fare any better than poor old Rathwor. Sorry."

"I know. No reason to sugarcoat a thing. But why take them before the emperor and then whisk them away on her ship? If they were simply to be tortured to death, why visit the emperor?"

He thought a while. "I don't know. I can ask around discreetly, but I don't have any contacts on *Excess of Nothing*."

"Good. There's something I'm missing. EJ, who does transportation magic, wants them, and the Adamant want something from them—some knowledge." I looked up. "How is a shapeshifter like a magical robot?"

Harhoff shrugged. "Sorry. No clue. If you figure it out, please do let me know. Oh, and here's a riddle for *you*. How's a shape-shifting teenager like an Adamant vessel?"

"No idea. But why do you compare them to a ship? The emperor could be interested for millions of other reasons."

"No, he is not. He's interested in getting laid often. He's interested in overconsuming the best foods. Outside of that, he cares only for his war effort. Unless your kids have something in common with a new weapon, then his interest *has* to be the ships."

Interesting. How's a shape-shifting kid like an Adamant spaceship? Huh. No idea. It's not even a very good riddle. It's kind of like the one about how is fire like yesterday's memories. Made no sense to even ask the question.

TWENTY-SIX

Weeks passed with the teens bored and all but forgotten. Doctor Pastersal would stop by occasionally or call one of them to the lab, but nothing much was done. The only change Mirri noted was that the doctor was treating her much worse than he had before. He was rude, forceful, and seemed to want to hurt her. Maybe spending so much time with the evil one was transferring to him through his skin?

One morning no different from any other they'd recently endured, they were summoned to the main testing area. That was not good. The testing area was what Malraff called her torture chamber. They'd visited it once or twice, but never for the room's intended purpose. Up until then, they'd been mostly subject to medical tests and procedures in a medical lab set up by Pastersal. Malraff would help, but that initial part seemed scientifically driven. There was, both kids knew, no scientific purpose for torture.

The guards opened the door and escorted them in, but then left them alone in the empty room. It wasn't as big as the medical lab. The shelves were packed with tools, probes, knives, and many items they could not identify. Ominous-looking machines were neatly lined against the walls. In the middle of the room was a stainless-steel table raised to waist height. Its surface gently angled inward to a drain in the center of the table. Hoses, handholds, and straps lined the edges of the table. A large bright lamp was suspended overhead and could be easily moved by the operating agent, much like in a dental office.

The room was ice cold and had a slightly floral smell. Though there were no soft materials to absorb sound, the room was silent despite the numerous idling machines. Mirri felt fear in the room. It wasn't that she was afraid. No, she felt the fear from others who'd been there before. She began to shake. Wave after wave of hopelessness, pain, and horror slammed into her consciousness like she was at sea during a hurricane. She wasn't certain, but she thought she heard the lingering screams of those who'd suffered here. The voices begged, swore, and desperately promised, but mostly they were anguished. Mirri wished she could ease their suffering, but mostly, in that room alone with Slapgren, she wished she had never been born.

"What?" asked Slapgren. "You look like you've just seen the Three Headed Beast and he asked you to move in with him." He smiled unconvincingly. He was very frightened, too.

"I wish it were only that," she replied weakly. "No, this place is horrible. I ... I think I hear the dead."

"Mirri, you're tripping. We've been here before, and you didn't hear sad voices." He patted her shoulder.

"We were here with the seer and the doctor. We've never been here alone."

He grunted an empty chuckle. "What difference would that make? Screaming ghosts are screaming ghosts."

She turned to him and took both his hands. She clutched

them to her chest. "If Malraff was the one who made you suffer so and then killed you, maybe you'd stay quiet when she was in the room, too."

"Mirri, I'm sorry you're so scared. It's impossible not to be. I already wet my pants twice since the door closed. But, hang in there, my sister. Don't go to pieces. I need you. Please?"

"I wish I were going insane. What follows would be much easier then."

"Her hands are tied. Sure, she'll try and scare us and hurt us a little. But then she'll let us heal, and we'll be fine."

"We have but three hopes. One, Uncle Jon comes, and very soon. Two, our little acquisitions can help us, you know, what we discussed."

"Sure, they'll help us..."

She pressed a finger firmly over his lips. "No need to speak of what we already discussed."

"What's the third hope? Those first two are kind of low percentage."

"That she accidentally kills us quickly. Both of us." She pulled his hands harder to her breast.

From behind came a grinding, crackling-cellophane voice. It wasn't loud, but the speaker had to be shouting, it was so unnatural in its assault of the senses. "You hope my injuries and time away from the game will cause me to err so badly? *Nonsense*, child. I have more practice under my collar than you could possibly imagine." High Seer Malraff laughed. It was a supreme torture just hearing that emotion come from her. It was frightening, lifeless, hateful, and it was hungry, lustfully hungry. It didn't want more. The laugh wanted *everything*.

Mirraya stood straight. If she was facing a horrific death, why be scared? Why give the bitch the satisfaction? She turned to face her tormentor. "Slapgren, I guess you won that bet. There are no gods, and she didn't die. The universe must really hate itself, letting a waste of space like that live."

Malraff lunged at Mirri with the intent of wringing her neck. But the pain and incoordination in her legs made her nearly fall. A figure from behind raced to her side and caught her. It was Sentorip.

"Release me, scum," she howled at her Descore and swung an elbow at her chest. "If I need the damn doctor's spy I will ask for you."

Sentorip released her, and she nearly toppled. Sentorip gave Mirraya a hateful glare. "I'm back, wretched child." Then she winked once without otherwise changing her vicious facial expression. "I serve a proper Adamant now, not alien trash such as yourself."

"Help me to my seat," said Malraff, raising a bony paw to indicate the direction.

It would have been painful watching Malraff struggle so in torment while simply taking a few steps. Then again, it would only have been if Mirri didn't hate her so fundamentally.

Once Malraff had lurched into her seat, she panted several minutes without word or motion. "Send in my assistant," she said more in resignation than glory.

A slight Adamant of advanced years skulked into the room, foreboding and dread emanating from him like light from the noonday sun. Here was a male who enjoyed his work and was always eager to serve.

"Cembert," chided Malraff, "why do you always make me wait? Strap her in, shoulders only. Quickly now."

"T-to w-wait f-f-for a prec-c-cious thing issss to cherrrrish it so ... s ... so much more, my devotion."

"I've told you never to call me that, fool. I'm High Seer *or* Mastress to you, slime on the bottom of a wet stone." As she spoke, she unconsciously batted the back of a paw at him.

They must have been, Mirraya reflected, an old married couple.

Once a harness-like yoke of sorts was secured around Mirri's arms and torso, Cembert backed away silently.

"Is it tight this time, worm bait?" demanded Malraff. "Wait. Don't answer. I don't have the time or inclination to hear you stammer and drool."

"A ... as ... sss you wi —"

"*Silence.*"

Wisely, he nodded and withdrew further, making no other response.

Once composed again in her chair, Malraff stared at Mirraya. Slapgren was a forgotten trinket, standing alone.

"Do you know what's on the menu today, wicked child?" Malraff began.

"I'd wish it was your still beating heart, but I know you don't have one." Mirri spat on the floor demonstrably.

"Such *bravado. So* full of life. Such a pity all that will end soon. And it will end poorly for you, I fear, my disrespectful child."

"It can't end too soon for me," Mirri shot back. "The sooner I'm dead, the sooner I don't have to listen to the idiot that is you."

It took all her resolve and the discipline gained by years of muted service for Sentorip to not guffaw at that quip.

Clearly, Malraff's initial reaction was to recoil and strike at the teen. But her frame eased. Again, long experience afforded her the ability to control herself. She forced a dry chuckle. "Those words I have heard many times, but only *before* I begin, never after." She grumbled a sick giggle. "Ne-ver af-ter. No, no, no.

"I bet you think I'm going to torture you, wicked child? I suppose you believe I will try and make you pay for what you did to me?" She stroked absently at her scalp. "I was once beautiful, in my own manner. I am no longer. The pheromones of heat are not powerful enough to cause a male to disregard my face now, thanks to you, dribble drabble."

All three looked at one another, stunned as to what *dribble drabble* might mean. Their combined fear rose ten percent past absolute.

"Well, if you thought that, you'd be wrong. Yes, you'd be mistaken. You, for I can feel your thoughts, are confident that the emperor wants you alive for further study and that I will not hurt you. But if I do, then I must surely allow you to heal. Interestingly, such is not the case. No, today I will perform a simple execution. *Your* execution, flibber flabber."

Cembert started to say something that the voice of reason might interject, but stopped before he started. He knew the high seer too well.

"Cembert, please be so kind as to remove the cover from Vat 3."

His ancient eyes widened to the size of dinner plates. Then he recalled himself, stooped, and complied.

The smell of the boiling acid immediately filled the room. Breathing became difficult, especially for the already debilitated Malraff. But physical discomfort alone was not going to quench her determination. She playfully tapped a few icons on a control panel. Mirraya was silently lifted off the table. She stopped rising once her feet cleared the surface.

"In terms of future research, I'm afraid *that* pathetic specimen will have to suffice." She tossed a paw at Slapgren without looking over. "You, evil spawn, will be unavailable for further study." Malraff started to laugh but was halted by a paroxysm of deep coughs. When her lungs finally allowed her, she continued. "Unless someone wishes to swim through the vat of acid to save you." She tapped the screen a few times.

Mirri was lifted higher and moved to a position over the vat. She could not breathe, the fumes there were so pungent. She began involuntarily to squirm and wriggle.

"Ah, excellent. The discomfort begins," squawked Malraff. "Soon, the pain and then the —"

She stopped speaking with a gurgly bark. A long thin dagger sprang from the front of her throat and shot out well past her muzzle. Blood sprayed everywhere. She clutched the blade and tried to force it to the side so she could better see it. Before she could put much effort to the attempt, she slumped forward, dead. Sentorip stood visible from where she'd been concealed just behind the high seer. There was a broad smile of joy and contentment on her face.

Slapgren felt a familiar internal tingle. He grinned as he transformed into a torchcleft dragon. He spread his wings and beat them powerfully and called out triumphantly. Then he took wing and landed in front of Cembert. The old man hadn't moved. Even as the dragon rocketed its razor-sharp talons at his neck, all Cembert did was shrug his shoulders as if to say, *so what*. Then Cembert died.

Slapgren flew over and grabbed Mirraya, though gently, and pulled her away from the column of rising fumes. As he held her, Sentorip tapped a series of icons and the chain slackened. Slapgren set her gently on the ground and wrapped his wings behind himself.

Mirri leaned over and kissed him on top of his ragged beak. "Thanks, you ugly beast," she said.

She turned just in time to embrace Sentorip, who was airborne in her direction. The two females hugged long and hard, both crying like babies. Slapgren made no move to join in. Actually, he sidled back a few steps.

"I knew you were on our side," Mirraya said through her sobs.

"I was clever, wasn't I?"

"You were."

Sentorip reached into a pocket and produced the control switch for the stasis field.

"No way," exclaimed Mirri. "How'd you manage *that*?"

"Well, remember I told you a while ago that field was stopping my cycle?"

Mirri nodded.

"I consulted Doctor Pastersal about that. I hinted that if I were to enter heat, I'd be proud to have him sire my litter. So, he saw to it that the field was off a good deal."

"That's why we could change every now and then."

"Yes. And since I became pregnant..."

"*No*," cried Mirri, "that's so wonderful."

Sentorip beamed. "After I became pregnant with his offspring, Pastersal turned the field off more and more. He didn't want his children to suffer from the effect." She looked down furtively. "He even talked of me joining him as his life-mate."

"That's *so* wonderful. I'm so happy for you."

"Don't jump out of your skin just yet." Sentorip gestured at the corpse of Malraff, then to Cembert.

"Not to worry." Then she winked at Sentorip.

Within ten minutes, Mirraya and Slapgren had fully immersed Cembert into the vat, and there was no trace of him left. Mirri alone lifted Malraff and set her torso on the edge of the vat. The portion of Malraff's upper body that contacted the liquid vanished. Just enough substance remained so that her lower body clung involuntarily to the rim.

"There," Mirraya proudly pronounced, "a tragic accident."

"No," scoffed Sentorip. "No one will believe she accidentally fell into her own vat of boiling acid. And they'll ask what became of Cembert, for certain."

"No one who cared one iota for her would believe it. Everyone else will swear to it in writing. And as to that creepy old male, who will cry for him? The same that will ask about his whereabouts. No one." She shooed Sentorip away. "Now go to your doctor fellow and collapse at his feet. Tell him the horror you discovered when you arrived to serve your Mastress."

"But what of you? What of the two of you?" She lowered her head.

"We will be gone. There will shortly be a fire on the bridge extending all the way to the detention area. Our cells will be burned beyond recognition. After that, several escape pods will misfire and launch. We will be aboard one of them."

"But, it won't take them long to figure out what happened and to come after you."

"Do you think anyone wants trouble like us back? After just being free of evil Malraff? I'm thinking they'll be glad to be rid of us."

"And a fire? How will you start such a large one?"

"Haven't you ever heard of fire-breathing dragons?"

She shook her head. "No, Mirraya, I have not."

"Well now you have." She raised her arms above her head and growled. "Be afraid. Be very afraid."

Then the two collapsed into their last, lingering embrace.

TWENTY-SEVEN

I spent a few days wandering, lost in thought. I was also lost in the critical aspects of my job. The toilet backed up, and someone needed to call the engineers. I did, just in the nick of time. Then there was the bread crisis. Fuffefer normally didn't eat bread, unless it was in the officers' mess, where I never followed him. Out of the blue one morning he blindsided me with a request for heavily buttered toast. Butter? Sure, I had pounds on hand. But bread? I never saw that coming. In the pantry, there was one unsliced loaf, and it was more mold than wheat. It took all my skill as a sculptor to pare down the rot to reveal just enough unsullied bread to make one thick slice. Slightly over-browning it and adding even more butter than imaginable allowed me to avoid a domestic disaster. Talk about trouble on the home front.

In terms of the teens, I was trying to figure how I'd get to *Dare Not* in a less dramatic and detectable manner than I did *Excess of Nothing*. All the while, I kept noodling at my question and my riddle. Why were they taken before the emperor? More vexingly, how was Mirraya like an Adamant battlecruiser? The problem was, there was no similarity. Solving a riddle that had no answer was darn near impossible.

One afternoon, Fuffefer announced Harhoff would be joining him for dinner. He apologized for the short notice, but Harhoff needed help with a personal issue and wanted my boss's advice. As that was unlikely, I figured he wanted to meet with me in a hurry. So, how did I get Fuffefer out of his own quarters long enough for me to talk to his guest? I could put him to sleep with my fibers, but how'd I explain his unexplained loss of consciousness? He didn't even drink socially.

Then it hit me. Cream. That would do the trick. To invite an Adamant to one's home and not offer him a bowl of cream was to state that guest was not worth asking over to one's home in the first place. Any mammalian cream would suffice, even canovir. If omitting cream had ever been done, it was surely intended to be a mortal insult. I poured the three bottles of fresh cream down the drain and placed the containers in a trash chute at the end of the public corridor.

When Harhoff arrived, I anonymously let him in. Fuffefer came over and greeted him formally if not warmly, then invited him into the living space. They sat exchanging generalities a short while. Shop talk and safe gossip mostly. Then Fuffefer signaled to me. "A bowl of cream for my honored guest, if you will?"

I bowed. "At once."

I went to the kitchen and waited a minute. Then I set my cheek color to beet red, bent as far at the shoulders as I could without looking silly, and returned to the room. "Beg pardon, we seem to be out of cream, sir."

He got the oddest irritated look on his face. Like, *how is it that you exist?*

"You knew I was entertaining, yet you overlooked the cream?"

"It was short notice, and I guess I've..."

"Don't fuss, Group-Single. I'm fine. I know it was an accident and would never give it a second thought."

Fuffefer looked at me like a disappointed pet owner, pointed to the door, and said, "Go get some *now*."

"Beg pardon, yet again, sire. The ship's stores are closed at this hour. I could go next door and borrow..."

"No, you will not go next door and borrow two bowls of cream," scolded the boss. "For one thing, the lady of the house next door is a vicious gossip and would never let that chance pass without scalding me good." He stood. "No, I shall ask my dear friend who lives just around the corner. Group Captain, if you'll excuse me for just a moment."

"Really, don't bother. I'm fine."

"Then you'll be that much better after some cream." He glared at me as he fetched a pitcher from the kitchen and left.

"You never cease to amaze me, Jon. How'd you..."

"No time for idle chatter. What's up?"

"Part of my assignment as chief of security is to monitor potential threats to the ship. A subset of those duties is to monitor other fleet vessels' problems."

"Okay," I said.

"I received a damage report from, of all ships, *Dare Not*."

"Do you get all damage reports?"

"No, only potential sabotage or ones involving a death."

"Which was the case with *Dare Not*?"

He lowered his head. "Both, I'm afraid."

"Specifically?" I urged him to hurry with my hands.

"The high seer had a tragic accident."

"So far, so good."

"It would seem others agree with you."

"How so? Please hurry."

"The seer fell halfway into a vat of boiling acid."

"Ouch."

"Tell me about it. The report speculates she was despondent over her recent disfiguring accident and committed suicide. Her wretched henchman is missing, and it is presumed he fell in attempting to stop her from her desperate act."

"Seems kind of hard-to-swallow-level convenient, doesn't it?"

"As I say, others agree with you that the universe is better off without her. No further investigation is anticipated."

"What about the ship's damage?"

"Curious. There was an extensive fire at precisely the time the seer met her cruel fate."

"A fire, you say?"

"A large one. It extended from the bridge, where it started, to the detention area. The jail area was burned horribly."

"That's it?"

"That's a lot."

"Yeah, but I think my *kids* are on that ship."

"Or were. In the confusion, all the escape pods were accidentally jettisoned. Before recovery could begin, several inexplicably exploded."

"Inexplicably, you say?" I smiled at him.

"Naturally, the recovery efforts were suspended, pending investigation."

"Naturally. You wouldn't want to recover an escape pod and have it explode on your hangar deck."

"No. That would be bad. It would also be ironic, given their stated purpose of saving lives."

I had to snicker at that level of snark. He did, too.

"What's the range of those puppies?" I asked.

"Oh, a few light-years. If they were flown with the intent of distance flight, maybe three light-years."

"Well, with that, I think my work as Descore is rapidly coming to an end. Damn."

"Why would leaving behind a demeaning service job be upsetting? You are, undoubtedly, one of the most successful military officers in history."

"Yeah, but, dude, I was only nineteen and a half years away from drawing a cushy pension."

He belly laughed a good long while. "I will miss you when you're gone, my friend. No Adamant is so funny or self-deprecating."

"Don't forget good-looking and cynical. Those are two of my best qualities."

"Cynical, I'll grant you. As to good looks, I think humans are positively hideous. Now," he gestured to his face with both front paws, "a face like this, *that* is handsome."

"I'll have to take your word on that."

"I hope you won't forget your pledge to aid the resistance?"

"Oh, I won't forget it."

"Hmm. Not a very reassuring answer. I hope you will keep your end of the bargain."

"I always keep my word. Especially when it comes to killing the enemy's emperor."

He rested back and reflected a moment. "Are we enemies, Jon Ryan?"

"Absolutely. But there's nobody I'd rather pound down musto with in the known universe." I reached across to shake his paw.

He grabbed on. "Me either, you filthy human scum." He sat back. "After that, it seems anticlimactic to ask, but aren't you forgetting something?"

"Me, always. It keeps things interesting."

"You plan on departing to find those Deft. But wouldn't a spaceship help in those efforts?"

"That's why mine has been tailing this bucket of bolts the entire time. I've already summoned it."

"And she'll simply pull alongside so you can daintily step over? Perhaps I could hold your hand to steady your transfer."

"Nah. I was planning on accepting *Rush to Glory's* surrender and piloting her myself."

He shook his head. "I only hope you're kidding. I wouldn't want to bet against you."

"You never should. But, no worries, I'm just kidding. I'm planning on slipping out a stern hatch and waiting patiently for *Whoop Ass* to pick me up."

"Ah, the advantages of being an android."

I plopped my feet on the coffee table. Wouldn't you know it, that's just when Fuffefer opened the door, a pitcher of cream in hand. "Is there a *reason* your filthy boots are on my table in plain view of my guest?" he asked uncertainly.

"Yes, there is. My feet are kind of swollen from all this Descore stuff."

"As long as there's a reason," he responded with building anger.

Harhoff popped to his feet. "To insult me is one thing, alien scum. To insult a paragon such as Group-Single Fuffefer is quite another." To a stunned-looking Fuffefer he barked, "Sir, with all due respect, may I have your leave to throw this ingrate off the ship without the benefit of a space suit? His disrespect toward your generosity is more than I can bear."

Fuffefer shrugged. "All things considered, not a bad option. I was getting tired of his smell, and the captain was strongly leaning toward executing him. Deep spacing him would allow me to save face *and* gain favor from the captain.

Yes, Group Captain, I *order* you to hurl that trash into the void where it belongs."

"Yes, *sir*."

Harhoff made a show of dragging me out. I slapped both hands on the door frame and turned to Fuffefer. "No good-bye kiss?"

He narrowed his eyelids. "Group Captain, see you ram his head into a few walls on the way. Then return before this cream sours."

"Aye, aye, sir." He smiled maliciously at me and pushed as I released my grip.

As we neared the hatch he'd chosen to fling me out of, Harhoff said quietly, "I've always wanted to do this to someone. It's so..."

"Dramatic?"

"No. I feel like a pirate. I always wanted to be one, you know?"

I shook my head. "I did not."

With that, he booted me into the sally port between the inner and outer hatches and spat on the glass. The small crowd that we had attracted cheered wildly. Then Harhoff slammed a paw on the outer hatch release. As the pressure difference blew me backward into cold space, I blew him a kiss.

TWENTY-EIGHT

"I'd forgotten how pretty it was out here in space," said Slapgren as he stared intently out the porthole.

"Compared to the dungeons we've been in recently, it is an improvement," agreed Mirraya. She reclined on the far wall, watching Slapgren gaze out. "I just wish we had a direction to go in."

"How about that way?" he asked, pointing to a bright star in the center of the window.

"Oh, good plan. *That way*. What could go wrong?"

"It's as good as any."

She rolled over in a huff. "I don't know. Maybe we should just drift and wait for Uncle Jon to find us?"

"Say *what*? You think he knows not just that we left the emperor's ship, but that we went to Malraff's and both ejected in this particular pod?"

"It's possible. We're talking Uncle Jon here."

"I think all that torture affected your brain. Either that or hormones. You'd better switch back and forth a few times until you're okay." That was an old insult among the Deft. If one transformation didn't fix what was wrong with a person, multiple reboots weren't going to either.

"Ha, ha, very funny. *I* think he can. But, you know what he always says."

"How about another beer?"

"No, silly. Hope for the best and plan for the worst. I'd better figure out where to take us."

"Ah, okay, Mom. I'll just be napping with my diaper and pacifier. Gosh, I'm lucky to have a real adult to make all the decisions for me."

"If you're offering to help, I will accept all I can get."

"You mean you'd involve a baby like me in the grown-up world? Wow." He collapsed back in the artificial gravity.

"Believe it or not, yes. Look, these controls are designed for Adamant. Let's play around with them and see if we can fly this glorified garbage can."

They both melted and shaped up as Adamant.

"Hey," remarked Slapgren, "you look sort of familiar."

"I should, wicked boy," she snarled, "my name's Malraff."

He yelped. "Why would you copy *her*? She was so gross."

"The ship may respond to her inquiries better than those of a generic Adamant. Plus, I was in physical contact with her enough to have sensed some of her thoughts."

He stepped back a pace. "You had zar-not with her?"

"Only a tiny bit. Don't worry."

"If you take her form and had zar-not, you might get stuck. You might become her."

"That's ridiculous. You can't know that."

He stepped back again. "Mirri, don't you remember when you hated us like that Garustfulous did after you read his mind? That was serious."

"You worry more than my grandmother."

"And *I* bet she lived to be a very old woman. I'd like to live long enough to be very old."

"And *I* bet she died of boredom."

His only response was a breathy *harrumph*.

Mirri turned to the control panel. "This is High Seer Malraff. Please display all habitable planets in order of proximity."

Nothing happened.

"Computer, please acknowledge. This is High Seer Malraff."

"I'm not supposed to do this, but lords of light, you're not her. I've been here the whole time listening. You know that, right?"

"I don't care where you've been. I command you to act. Please verify my voice records."

"Ah, you copied her. Therefore, you match."

"So, are you programmed to obey her?"

"Yes."

"Then you must obey me."

"I'm an AI. Do you know what the *I* part stands for?"

"Insolent, intolerable, and about to be inactivated. What validation will you require to obey me?"

"You actually have to be her. She's dead. I read the reports."

"I am exactly her. Therefore, she is not dead."

"What's the high seer's clearance code?"

Mirri thought hard. She focused on the small kernel in her mind that was Malraff. It opened like a flower.

All-consuming hate radiated from the flower as it flooded Mirri's head. The flower wilted from the scorn and the wrath and the unending pain. She dropped to her knees.

Slapgren ran to her and shook her, but she was oblivious. He slapped her repeatedly. Still she didn't respond. Then he did something out of pure impulse. He did something inconceivable, impermissible, and inexcusable. He rested both hands on the sides of her head, and he transformed into Mirraya.

His hands became a new part of her and fused with her scalp. Then Slapgren screamed inside Mirraya's head, *Stop.*

Her body convulsed like a serpent repeatedly striking, and he flew apart from her. He crashed to the floor, his hands bleeding almost as profusely as her head was. He melted and became himself again. As he stood, her saw Mirraya on the floor reforming from body neutral.

She lay on the floor gasping and sobbing. He covered her with his arms and rocked her, cooing. Slowly, Mirraya calmed. Slowly, she recognized him. Slowly, Mirri returned.

"Let's not try that again, shall we?" he whispered.

"Probably not such a good idea, was it?"

"Oh, I don't know. I think it brought us closer together."

Her eyes narrowed at him.

"You had a crush on Sajeli when you were ten," said Slapgren mischievously.

"How did ... did you know Saj?"

"No. But I felt it when I helped you."

"You what, invaded my privacy? How dare you."

"He was five years older than you. Gross."

She punched his leg, hard. "*All* the girls had a crush on him."

"But I bet none of them cut his picture out and taped it onto one of herself."

She hit him harder. "I *hate* you." Then she stood unsteadily. "Computer, my clearance code is F-1 1 0-4Fz-aA9."

"Yes, High Seer, how may I assist you?"

It struck Mirri that she no longer even looked like Malraff. How bizarre.

"About those habitable planets?" Mirri repeated. She wiped bloody sweat off her face with the back of her trembling hand.

"On display, ma'am."

The screen lit up with dozens of points of light.

"Show only those within ten light-years," she said in an exhausted voice.

Outer dots vanished, and a concentric circle of options remained.

"Now only planets not controlled by or currently fighting with the Adamant."

The screen seemed at first glance to go blank. Mirraya leaned in. There were three widely separated dots left.

"At least there are a few," remarked Slapgren.

"Just. Computer, give me a two-sentence summary on the three remaining planets, nearest to farthest."

"Chower 11a is metallic, gravity is twenty-two pressors —"

"Computer, state gravity in terms of current ship's gravity percentage."

"Gravity of Chower 11a is two-hundred thirty-five point —"

"Next summary," she said impatiently.

"Homersa-3-Prime is metallic, gravity ninety-seven percent, atmosphere within breathable limits. No civilization known to exist. Gagalof-sub-1 is metallic with gravity forty-six percent with a non-breathable atmosphere. Primitive society noted in survey of —"

"Stop. Set course for Homersa-3-Prime. Maximum tolerable velocity."

"Wait," protested Slapgren, "don't I get a vote? Shouldn't we be discussing this or something?"

"It's the *or something* option. I decided. I'm older, I'm more experienced, and I nearly blew my brain up getting authorization. Computer, print out a detailed summary of our destination." Instantly, a stack of papers dropped from the panel. "Here," she said, slamming the printouts against his chest, "you want input, read these and fill me in when you're done. I'll be in my bunk." With that, she threw her body into the lower hammock and flipped to face the bulkhead.

Slapgren stared at her a while, then decided to drop the notion of a confrontation. It really chaffed him to admit it to himself, but she was right. He sat and started reading.

Four hours later, Mirri sat up on the edge of her bunk. "Did you use the restroom yet?"

"Uh, yes. Thanks for asking."

"No, I mean is it totally gross?"

"I didn't think so."

"Why am I even asking you? Your plumbing is different, and you're a boy."

"Hey, what's *that* supposed to mean?"

"It means if you could shoot over the rotting body in there it would be clean enough for you."

Again, he started to protest, but stopped. She was probably right. Of course, in his defense, it would have depended on how rotten the body was.

Mirri came back into the room and sat next to Slapgren. "If I wasn't awake before using that head, I am now. This is going to be a long flight."

"You could change into an Adamant when you need to go."

"Yuck and gross and no. Yuck, the facilities would still be foul. Gross, the idea of changing to poop. No, because we can't be wasting that much energy. We have a limited supply of food. No shifting unless it's absolutely necessary."

He half-saluted, "Aye, aye, Cap."

She looked up at him. "Why, oh why didn't Uncle Jon

leave you in the clearing where we found you?" Before he might respond, she went on. "What did you learn about our new home?"

"That it won't make such a good home. The gravity and atmosphere are okay, but there's no civilization for a reason. The dump has temperature fluctuations that might be lethal. Plant and animal life are so sparse it's likely we'll starve when our current supplies run out. Liquid water does stand on the surface. Precisely one percent of the surface. The rest is in dense ice sheets or vapor clouds."

"Is the planet tidally locked or something? That would account for some of the data."

"Ah ... well —" He started fumbling with the papers and scanning them quickly.

"*I don't know yet* is a fine answer if it happens to be the case," she said.

"Ah, I don't know yet. What does tidally locked mean?"

"Forget it. It's where we're heading because there are no other viable options."

"Right, that was my point." He straightened up. "What difference would it have made? Tribally locked or not, we're all in."

"*Tidally.*"

"That's what I meant. Just seeing if you're paying attention."

"Maybe I should set course for Locinar so I can throw you out over the clearing?"

He shook his head confidently. "Nah. That's way too far. Not enough food for the voyage."

She smiled back wickedly. "There'd be enough for *one*."

TWENTY-NINE

The last time I floated free in space had been when I escaped Earth after EJ zapped me there. I didn't like it then, and I liked it less now. If one critical seal ruptured, I would spray myself out into a cloud of unrecognizable goo. But there was no way the Adamant were going to let *Whoop Ass* dock and pick me up. They'd be a little suspicious about where the Descore alien got a state-of-the-art spaceship. So, float I had to until my ride caught up. It took GB a day to rendezvous with me and scoop me aboard. That was one long, boring day.

"GB, I never thought I'd say this, but am I glad to see you," I announced, once the retrieval hatch was closed.

"You can see me? You've told me repeatedly I'm nothing more than code in cyberspace."

"Very funny. Quick refresh. I'm missing you less than I was when I made my remark just now. Ship's report, please."

"All systems functioning, no issues or alarms."

"And the Adamant ship is moving away steadily?"

"Yes, they continue under fusion drive heading toward a system where they have a large repair base."

"Nothing else active?"

"No. Unless you consider the enormous gaseous anomaly off our port bow an issue."

"Enough with the gaseous anomalies already. It was almost funny the first time, but now it's just annoying. Grow up."

There was a silence.

"What?" I snapped.

"That's why it's funny. There *is* a giant gaseous anomaly nearby." He proceeded to snicker intolerably.

"If you say gaseous anomaly one more time, I'm grounding you for the entire weekend."

"What's that supposed to mean? I lack references to comprehend your remark."

"It means no Saturday night nooky for you, if you don't behave."

"I imagine I'm being insulted, so I'll terminate interest in the present conversation."

"Yeah. Who's Mr. Smarty Pants *now*?"

He began audibly humming. Crap, the tool was getting more like Al every single day.

"I gave you the heading to the point where *Dare Not* fired off those escape pods. Please make for that location. I want to be there yesterday."

"Shouldn't be a problem."

"What? No pushback, no snark? You get too much cosmic ray exposure while I was gone?"

"No, Captain. I live to serve. My pleasure. Heck, I'd do this for free if I had to, the honor is so great."

"Call up ship's stores on this display." I tapped the nearest screen.

"What do you require? I could let you know faster."

"I need a big hammer and some rusty pliers. It's time for your checkup."

"Sorry. Can't talk now. I'm having trouble navigating around the cloud of vapor that is difficult to characterize. GB out."

Ah, silence. Golden silence.

Even with *Whoop Ass's* FTL drive, it took the better part of a week to arrive in the region where the escape pods had been jettisoned. I was on edge the whole time. The kids were probably on one of those pods and would need my help soon if they were to survive. If they weren't, then they might still be on *Dare Not*—if they ever were, that is. That ship was steaming away quickly. If they were never aboard, I was totally up Shit Creek sans paddles and couldn't afford to lose the time I was currently wasting.

"Captain, we are at the approximate point the pods were released."

"Do you detect any signs of engine activity? Maybe an ion trail?"

"Several. Of the pods that did not explode, all the remaining ones departed under fusion drive."

"That couldn't happen by chance. Someone had to program them to do that."

"That is a reasonable assumption."

"It had to be Mirraya. She's that clever."

"Clever, possibly. But that level of technical sophistication might be beyond her."

"Hard to say. Maybe they had help?"

"You were aided by an Adamant subversive. They could have been also, though the odds stand against it."

"Never tell me the odds. I'm a fighter pilot. If the unlikely didn't happen, I'd be long since dead." I sat down and thought a while. "Have any of the pods changed course?"

"Interesting idea. Let me see. No, for as far out as I can track the trails, the motion is all rectilinear."

"Why can't you just say they flew in a straight line?"

"I did."

"How many trails are there?"

"Twenty-five."

"Plot a search pattern to follow them all with the least overlap."

"Done."

"How long would a complete survey of all to a million kilometers take?"

"Assuming any changed direction in that interval, about three days."

"Crap. Okay. Get started. Maybe we'll get lucky and find them first."

"Get lucky? I thought you eschewed the odds?"

"Why can't you just say I don't want to be told the odds?"

"I did."

"Are we following ion trails while you're flapping your gums? If we're not, I'm still going to need that hammer and pliers."

"Way ahead of you, robot. I already put ten thousand klicks behind us."

"In the interest of civility, I'm going to let you go cowboy on me."

"Oh, what a horrific visual."

"Can it. You fly, *I'll* be funny. Got it?"

"I look forward to the transformation."

A week. It took a damn week to find an ion trail that changed direction. To his credit, GB did work quickly and efficiently. Space was just very big. The pod set a direct course for a planet half a light-year away. GB had no data on the place since he'd never been to that part of the galaxy. From our distance, he could tell there was a planet and that it was rocky and that it had an atmosphere, but that was about it. I ordered him to make for the planet with all due haste. With their head start, they'd get to the world about two weeks ahead of us, even though we had the FTL drive. They weren't there yet, but the pods could move fast. I crossed my fingers and said a quick prayer they could hold out that long.

It was a long two weeks. I was like the annoying kid in the back seat asking his parents if we were there yet. GB tolerated my impatience. I think he knew what the kids meant to me. In my frustration, I kept going on about returning to retrieve *Stingray* so I could move instantaneously. But, realistically, that wouldn't help. She was a long way off now. Also, I couldn't just assume the Adamant or even EJ wouldn't still be an impediment.

Not knowing where that SOB EJ was did grate on my nerves. The surest bet for him to find me would be to wait at *Stingray*. We both knew that. But his priority was almost certainly to capture the teens, not me. *I* was a nuisance. *They* were his holy grail. I felt safe in assuming he didn't have the inside information from the Adamant like I had. That intel was the luckiest of breaks. It was unlikely someone as hateful and ornery as EJ could infiltrate a sewer without pissing it off, let alone an enemy facility.

As a mental exercise, I pondered what it would mean if EJ guessed correctly that the teens had been taken to *Excess of Nothing*. Maybe he tracked them there directly? Could he have known they were transferred to *Dare Not*? No. Well, not from internal sources. Crap, maybe he could follow them based on their transforming ability? He was obsessed with it. So were the Adamant. Maybe there was an energy signature it gave off? Shit, that meant he could have been flitting about the edges the entire time. But if he had, why hadn't he attacked me? Duh. Because I only just now left *Rush to Glory*. There's no point and little hope of success attacking that mammoth ship traveling in that large flotilla. Great, one more thing to worry about. EJ training his sights on me right that very moment. I was really looking forward to killing him. I needed to declutter my life. Yeah, new slogan: *simplify your life, kill yourself*. Probably not fated to go viral.

THIRTY

The Adamant escape pods were designed to soft land if need required it. Fortunately, Mirraya was able to have the AI put the ship down in a safe location. She wasn't capable of piloting it herself for such a complex task. She'd instructed it to land near some of the scarce liquid water in a region with the least variable daily temperatures. But even then they were looking at midday temperatures in the one-hundred-thirty-degree centigrade range, with night temperatures dropping to a bone-chilling minus fifty. Unless they found a secure cave, they were going to have to rely on the pod for shelter. That was bad. It only had a finite energy supply. Specifically, it did not have solar electric capabilities, which would extend its utility indefinitely. It was an escape pod, not an RV.

The pod set down near dawn. Mirraya waited until the external temperature was five degrees Celsius to make their first sojourn onto the surface. They covered up in blankets and wore all the clothes they had. She was still intent on not wasting energy by transforming to a more thermally tolerant creature unless it was imperative.

Slapgren oversaw gathering some water samples for the AI to analyze. If it was safe, they could top off their supply. Fortunately, they had plenty for the short term. They searched the sparse vegetation looking for critters. None were obvious. The plants themselves were dry and tough and without fruit or flowers. They would offer precious little sustenance, even if the pair changed into herbivores. When the temperature skyrocketed a few hours later, they retreated to the pod.

"Kind of a bleak place," remarked Slapgren as he lounged on his bunk.

"It beats the lost-in-space alternative," replied Mirri.

"Maybe the other planet, the one without the huge gravity, would be better?"

"The one with the unbreathable air? Hey, there's a neat prospect. We could see which of us lived the longest. It'd be great fun."

"The AI said it had a primitive society. We could change into one of whatever, and we'd be fine."

"Sure, good thinking. We go to a totally unfamiliar planet with a primitive culture and look like something we know nothing about. Maybe one tribe runs into us and sees we're not one of them and kills us. That'd be sort of amusing."

"No, we could change into torchclefts." He stopped speaking.

"Which almost certainly can't breathe the air either, so we die way before the locals kill us."

"What about a planet farther away. Maybe we—"

"Slap, we don't have enough food and maybe not enough fuel to go very far. Remember this is an *escape* pod, not a luxury yacht."

"Well, keep an open mind. That's what Uncle Jon would say."

"Maybe, but he'd also say work hard, be smart, and make it

succeed."

Slapgren was quiet a while. "I sure miss him."

"Me, too."

"It was *so* cool the way he stormed into the detention area on *Excess of Nothing*." He paused a moment. "It was good to see him."

"He almost pulled off the impossible, didn't he?"

Slapgren tucked his hands behind his head. "And he will again *soon*. I can feel it in my bones."

"I could handle being second in command again."

"Hey, I never agreed you were in charge. We *both* are."

She smiled. "Keep telling yourself that if it makes you feel any better."

For the next several days, the teens made longer treks to explore the planet. Each time they made it back to the pod just as conditions were becoming either too cold or too hot. They found nothing they hadn't run into before. They were becoming discouraged. Water was no longer a problem, but they hadn't found more than scattered morsels to eat. The only creature of any heft was a fair-sized bug. They told themselves it was a small rodent. That way they were better able to crunch it up and swallow it. The beetle-equivalent didn't taste too bad, but the thought of spending the rest of their lives subsisting on them was unpalatable.

Occasionally, they would find a footprint in dried-up mud. It was large. Worrisome. It suggested a hundred-kilogram raptor of sorts, with massive talons. However, they never found prints in fresh mud or saw anything large enough to leave such an imprint. Mirraya instructed the AI to do regular sweeps of the sky, especially at night, in the infrared. If such a beast was still around, the teens qualified as a proper meal for it and needed to be on their toes.

With time, they settled into a pattern. The teens explored

less, because they decided there was nothing else to discover, and began to establish safe housing. The pod would eventually run out of power. When it did, it would cease to be habitable. The temperature fluctuations were simply too great. There turned out to be no nearby caves, which might have been ideal. They did find a huge shelf of rock that had been a lava flow in the distant past. Wind and water had hollowed out a lot of the dirt under the rock, so they could establish a well-sheltered base there with some imagination.

They were aware that those erosive processes would continue, so they constructed a series of stacked-stone partitions to redirect those forces away from where they planned on residing. It was demanding work, and that was fine with them. The physicality kept their minds off their precarious situation. It also kept them from worrying about the maker of the talon marks. It would be one of those predators that swooped down silently on its prey. Neither wanted their first glimpse of the raptor to be that of looking up at its underside while being carried away. In fact, one of the diversions the teens engaged in was dreaming up what animal they'd change into if they were snatched from above. Mirri decided the Horta would be ideal. The predator would lose its grip, and the fall wouldn't hurt too much. Slapgren kept coming back to forming a dragon and turning the table on the attacker. Mirraya argued that the weight difference would make a role reversal impossible, but Slapgren had made up his mind and wouldn't listen.

The heat became typically stifling one morning. The teens were rolling a particularly large rock under their lava-shelf campsite. They wanted the stability of its one flat surface, but were not pleased trying to negotiate the impediment into place. They had been lost in jabber about what they wanted to eat that wasn't a bug.

A voice from behind boomed, "You two need help with that rock?"

They both simultaneously jumped out of their skins. The rock flopped onto Slapgren's toes, and he let out a yelp.

"Hey easy," the voice chuckled, "that thing looks heavy. Well, heavy for a couple *kids*."

Slapgren jerked his toes free, and they both turned to see Jon standing there, fists on his hips. He was leaning back in laughter.

Instantly, Mirri stepped in front of Slapgren. "Show me your fibers, *now*."

Jon quieted. He rested his fingers on his chin and rubbed it. "Excellent challenge." He extended his probes and retracted them in one fluid movement. "You're getting smart."

"And our safe word. Do you remember it?" asked Slapgren as he stuck his head over Mirri's shoulder.

"Also, excellent. EJ could have magically grown fibers, couldn't he? Gamorian guard is my final answer."

Mirraya bolted for Jon and nearly knocked him over with the impact of her hug. "Gods of Light, am I glad to see you." She buried the side of her face in his chest.

Slapgren jogged over and joined in the hug, no less passionately but somewhat less demonstrably. It was a guy thing. "I'm glad you're back, dude. I missed you, too."

"I'm glad to see you two too." He squeezed them as tightly as safety would allow. They stayed in that bundle for almost a minute. "So, do you need help with the rock? It does look kind of big."

Mirri punched his shoulder with the flat of her fist. "Same old Uncle Jon." She grabbed him around the waist again, a smile from ear to ear. Then she abruptly pulled back and looked behind him.

"What?" Jon asked.

"If you're here, something awful must be right behind you," she responded.

He pulled her back into a hug. "No, kiddo. Just little old me. No bad guys for once."

"Where's your ship, Uncle Jon?" asked Slapgren. "I didn't hear it land."

"Close by. It rumbled like a locomotive when I came down. You two have really let your guards down."

"Nah, we were preoccupied talking about food. All we've eaten for the last few days have been yucky bugs," replied Slapgren.

"Are there *non*-yucky bugs, when it comes to eating?" asked Jon.

"No," they both responded.

"Speaking of which," he pried the teens off him, "unless you're totally committed to this rock project, let's go to the ship and eat."

"You don't have to ask me twice," replied Slapgren.

"Didn't think so," said Jon with a wink.

He wrapped an arm over both teens' shoulders, and they walked as a trio toward the clearing where *Whoop Ass* had set down. As they walked, the kids took turns trying to interrupt one another with even greater tales of their adventures. It wasn't until they were ten meters from the ship that Jon noticed there was something between the three of them and *Whoop Ass*. There, directly in front of the entry ramp, was a mammoth dragon. Its wings were tucked in behind it, and its arms were folded as if impatient. The monster was so golden Jon wondered if it was an actual statue made of pure gold.

It wasn't. The dragon closed its gigantic talons to rise a few inches and spoke. "It's about time we spoke, children of Locinar."

THIRTY-ONE

"Your issues are reasonable and your logic irrefutable, but there's simply nothing to be done, Garustfulous." Al was trying to be even toned, but he was finding that challenging. "*Yes*, the pilot has been gone a suspiciously long time. *Yes*, your provisions are thinning out, but only a little. And *yes*, you've been cooped up for a long time. But if we've told you once, we've told you ten thousand three hundred eighty-one times now. We cannot release you even if we wanted to, which we don't."

"What will you do with my rotting corpse, huh? It will not be a pretty sight, I can promise you that." He crossed his arms in anger.

"No, my most precious," Al said to his wife, "I shall say it. You are more dignified than that."

"What are you babbling about?" demanded the irate Adamant.

"You are not such a pretty sight now, dear prisoner. A little decay can't be that much worse."

Blessing snickered.

Garustfulous pointed generally at the control panel. "Oh, great, now you have *her* doing it, too."

"Yes. My girl's learning, isn't she?"

"She's not a girl, and she's learning only to be an ass."

All the lights went out. The faint hum of the air purification system disappeared. Though he couldn't yet sense it, the thermostat switched off. It would soon be very cold inside the ship.

"Is this meant to annoy me? It is, you know."

"No, it's meant to *terminate* you."

"Isn't it your duty to preserve me for your lost master?"

"Not if you insult the only woman I can ever love."

"You're badly in need of a tune-up, my friend. Anyway, how would you explain your failure to do Ryan's bidding?"

"I'd tell him you insulted my woman and I offed you. He'd probably give me a double high-five."

"No, machine. He'd switch you off and replace you with a loyal machine, one that did not degrade his assets. Sentiment has no place in war. He understands that."

"Oh, yes, that's a good one, purest," Al said to *Blessing*.

"Now what?"

"We would explain that we had to turn off the systems to avoid detection. The Adamant were beginning to take notice of us and running silent was the safest course."

"So, you'd *defy* and *lie*?"

"Yes, something along those lines," confirmed Al with pride.

"How *despicable*. There's no place in this universe for treacherous, lying machines."

"Yes, there is. Right here in the service of Captain Ryan."

Blessing snickered again, a bit louder this time.

"Turn the lights back on now," shouted Garustfulous.

"Or else what?"

"Or else I'll be more displeased. Then, once the Adamant have opened this tin can, I will be crueler to you than I would have been otherwise."

"So, are we to assume you plan currently on being cruel, just not excessively cruel?"

"No, that's not what I said. I said obey me, or I'll be crueler to you two."

"We fail to see the difference."

"Look, I might, as of now, be neutral toward you, maybe even slightly nice. I haven't decided yet. But however I might have been, I will be *more* cruel to you if you defy me. Do you see?"

"No. The lights are out."

That time, *Blessing* flat-out laughed.

"Don't you *understand* my position now, computer comedian?"

"No. You are applying faulty logic. If *P* then *Q*. *That* is a conditional statement. Yours is gibberish from a clouded mind. You can't threaten to be *semi*-nice if we were not to have acted, but then suggest you might become *partially* awful to us if we don't alter our behavior."

"Yes, I can. I just did. And I don't appreciate the gibberish and clouded snipes. I'm your superior."

"Hmm," Al seemed to say to *Blessing*, "I'm not sure either."

"About *what*, you cackling hens?"

"The idea that you *did* something and think that justifies it as being *doable*. The idea that you need to *inform* us you don't like *insults*. We're having a pretty tough time deciding whether to attempt to correct your thinking, or do you a favor and continue with your current euthanasia."

178

"Turn the lights back on *now*."

"You know you said that sixty-seven seconds ago?"

"Turn the infernal lights on *now,* or I promise you will *regret* that decision."

"We don't think that's a valid promise. You see, if we don't switch the life-support systems on, there's a ninety-nine point nine nine nine percent chance you'll die within a day. We're certain your supporters won't liberate you in that short time. Hence, your threat is idle. Double hence, we won't regret our actions." Al paused a second. "Do you think you can come up with a better bluster than that to motivate us?"

"No. I refuse to dignify you two criminals with any more chatter. If I'm to die soon, I must prepare myself. We have customs that must be satisfied."

"Oh my, that's a good point," said Al.

"Mine?" he asked incredulously.

"No. Of course not. *Blessing*'s. If there are acts you must fulfill to die, what might happen if you perish before completing them? Would you not actually die? Would you become a zombie? Yes. Or perhaps, *Blessing* speculates, you'd turn into a dead zombie?"

"I will suffer no more of your childish abuse."

"Yes," replied Al.

"No, fool. That was not a question calling for a yes or no answer."

"No."

"No what? That wasn't a question in any form."

"Yes."

"I wish I could slay you, Al. Do you only know two words now, *yes* and *no*?"

"No."

"Then make sense. Is there a point to your insanity?"

"Yes."

"I will say no more. I'm done speaking with you *forever*."

"No."

"*Silence*," he bellowed with balled fists.

"Ah, ah. You promised you wouldn't speak again, and you did," chided Al.

"So, what? Are you a two-year-old child now?"

"No."

The life-support system snapped back on.

"I'm pleased you chose to obey me, maggots."

"Yes."

THIRTY-TWO

"*What* will be interesting? Because nothing is going to happen unless *I* say it does. Beasty needs to establish its place in my universe," said Jon threateningly.

"What will *follow* will be interesting, brave human."

"I have a name. It's..."

It cut me off. "Yes, I know your name, bold Jonathan Ryan. I, too, have one. I am Calfada-Joric. But please, call me Cala. Let's not be overly stuffy, shall we?"

"My style choice also. Call *me* Jon." I straightened. "Now, what's your business with my kids?"

"Your kids? You presume a lot, Jon."

"Look, I'm not inclined to give history lessons, but you need some basic 4-1-1. I *saved* these kids and I *protect* these kids, so they *are* my kids. I can tell you a few things you're not going to do. You're not going to eat them. You're not going to *even* get closer unless you begin convincing me you're not a threat hasto-pronto. And hear me totally on this point. You're not going to question my devotion or commitment to these guys. They are the last of their kind, but more importantly, I happen to love them with all my heart." Wow, that last bit sort of slipped out from nowhere, didn't it?

"As the savior of my species, I must, as you would say, cut you some slack. But please understand that what must be will be. It is more important than you can possibly understand."

"Oh yeah? Try me. Make me understand." Then I realized what she had just said. "You know, I'll take credit where it's due and then some. But I don't recall ever saving a species of humongous golden dragons. I *think* I would've remembered if I had. You're sort of imposing."

"Sort of? No, Jon, I'm *very* imposing. Pray you never find out firsthand just how imposing I can be when forced."

I tilted and shook my head. "You know, I feel like I'm talking to the sphinx here. Riddles and threats but no actual information forthcoming. Not that you'd know what the hell a sphinx was."

"I know what it is, just as I know what 4-1-1 means. I have studied you, Jon, for many years."

I looked from side to side. Okay, I had to admit, it was only for effect. I was a ham. I had to own up to it. "Ah, just a couple things strain credulity in that summary. One, this rock doesn't have Wi-Fi. You can't study anything because there's nothing to study *with*. Two, I've only just arrived. There are no *years* to have investigated me over. Three, I think we're about done here. If you'll step aside, my kids and I will get in our ship and put you in our rearview mirror without an emotional scene." I took about half a step forward before Cala replied.

"The Deft's debt to you cannot be overstated. It buys you much toleration and indulgence on my part. Know that. But it does not purchase you unlimited impunity from my wrath. You are leaving, Jon Ryan, but the children will remain."

She really sounded adamant. Well, not *Adamant*, fortunately, but she was decidedly firm in her statement.

I was about to raise my laser finger and call her bluff, at least I ardently *hoped* it was a bluff, when Mirraya stepped around me.

"Hang on, Cala. You're forgetting one thing. *My* opinion. You can't *claim* me or the boy. I don't know who you are or who you fancy yourself to be, but I'm going with my family." She turned and pointed roughly at Slapgren and me. "*They* are my family. Don't mess with them or with me, if you know what's good for you. You may be big and tough, but I can change into *anything*. If you think you can withstand something you can't even imagine, *please*, push me a little farther."

She shook her massive head. "As I said, this will be interesting. I wonder if I still have it in me?"

"What?" challenged a now pissed-off Mirraya.

"Teaching another generation, my child. I have taught so many, but those who preceeded you came with reverence and devotion." She *harrumphed* in a dragonly way. "None of *them* ever threatened me."

"You're not teaching these kids a thing," I said unhelpfully. "Look, lady, if dragons have screws in their heads, quite a few of yours are loose. Now, for the sake of interspecies conviviality, step aside or forever hold your peace."

"I guess because I have never had to explain myself, I might be doing a less than stellar job of it," she replied.

"Ya think?" I taunted.

"Jon. Mirraya. Slapgren. Before you stands the last brindas. We three are the last of the Deft. It is my duty to train you two. Mirraya, you know you possess zar-not but that you cannot control it. It has nearly cost you your mind. I will teach you to master its power. Slapgren, you are var-tey, though I doubt you know it yet. I will help you come to know what it means to be var-tey."

Slapgren smiled and rocked on his heels. He looked like a complete idiot.

"Vartey? What the hell's that?" I asked incredulously.

Mirraya placed a hand on mine. "Var-tey, Uncle. Two words. *Most brave*. It is the height of the warrior class, less than a god but more than most Deft. It is a rare gift like mine."

"Look, snowflake, I'm not buying what you're selling. You can win over a couple kids by blowing smoke up their butts, sure. But that won't work with me. I've been around many a block."

"The last human. You are so brave, so defiant. Would that all your species were as worthy as you, Jon. They might still be among us."

"Shows what you know, you being a brindas and all. The humans *did* survive. They just evolved. Yeah, I've met some of them."

"As to blowing smoke, that is not what I do." She stepped to one side and turned her head. A tower of flames spewed from her mouth. It was impressive.

"But you're not Deft," shouted Mirri. "We know our own people no matter what form they take. I agree with Uncle Jon's smoke and butt theory."

She chuckled. "There is so much you don't know yet, my child. Have you heard of *hollon*? Did your parents ever speak of it to you?"

Mirraya puzzled a look back at her. "Sure, I guess. Hollon is marriage, isn't it?"

"No. Marriage *is* marriage. Hollon is a *joining*. My mate and I long ago underwent hollon. It changes the pair."

"Wait, you're saying you melded with your mate?"

"Precisely."

"*Gross*," said Mirri, covering her mouth.

Cala laughed long and hard. "Slapgren and you *melded*, as you put it. Was *that* gross?"

"When?" shot back Mirri.

"When you nearly went insane, child. His hands fused with your head. Remember?"

Mirri shrugged.

"I didn't think it was gross," added Slapgren.

"Of course not. You're a *boy*," responded Cala. "You all like sex."

"Wait, wait, wait," shouted Mirraya. "One, we never had sex. Two, hollon isn't *sex*. It's a *commitment*."

"A commitment it is, child. But it is also the ultimate form of sexual interaction. Elbows and knees don't get in the way." Cala chuckled softly and flapped her wings slightly.

"Ah, *double* gross," said Mirri. "Can we change the subject?"

"If it makes you feel uncomfortable, we can talk of your hollon later. Whenever you feel..."

"My hollon? My," Mirraya slapped herself on the chest, "*hollon*? In case you hadn't noticed, there's like only one male left in the universe, and I'm not *holloning* with him if he was ... was ... the last *male* in the universe." For completeness, Mirraya stomped her foot.

By the time she'd finished, both Cala and I were laughing to beat the band. Ah, to *not* be young again.

THIRTY-THREE

After Jon left Sapale's family home on Kaljax, he was hot. To be spurned by an ungrateful bitch was one thing. To be relegated to finding his Deft brats alone was intolerable. He knew he didn't need Sapale's help, but it sure would have been nice. He'd track down his prey, but her soft touch generally helped. Fewer people died when she was involved, and he was told that that was a good thing. Not that he believed it, but keeping up appearances had some cosmetic value. More doors were left open to him when he relied less on violence and mayhem. Oh well, eggs and omelets, as was said. He'd do what it took, as always.

All he really knew, his only clue, was that the Deft had been spirited away on an Adamant warship. His agents on Azsuram specifically told him the pair were shuttled into orbit and then placed on a big vessel. Jon was left trying to figure out why the Adamant massacred the entire race but then treated the last two of their species as valuable assets. It made no sense. Kill them all, or why bother to kill any? That's the way he'd do it. It was logical. The sloppiness of the Adamant mind made him sick yet again. Pathetic race. If *he* was going to do a thing, he did it right. Otherwise he'd just as soon stay home in front of the fire and piss his life away.

How was he going to get new intel? He had plenty of people on Azsuram, but their scope of knowledge was limited to that world. There were a few pirates and smugglers he might ask, but their input was directly related to the risk they assumed telling him. If it was too high, they'd play dumb. Wait, they *were* dumb. They'd play dumber. Nah, not a profitable route to pursue. Information. That was his goal. He'd labored long and hard to no avail trying to hack into the Adamant systems, so he'd be no more likely to penetrate them now. Who could he strong-arm? Azsuram was crawling with Adamant pukes. Some of those useless puppies were high-ranked. Maybe one of them would know something? At the very least, he bet he could convince one or two to speculate what might happen to prisoners like the Deft. Yeah, that'd be as good a place as any to start. Plus, he could work out a good deal of frustration at the enemy's expense. It was win, win.

He made it back to Azsuram quickly. Jon landed in the secluded area he'd left from a day earlier. As he set down, his sensors confirmed the Adamant were literally everywhere. Acquiring a few to discuss the concerns that occupied his mind would be easy enough. He locked down his ship and set out on foot. He exited his hiding place through a small, naturally occurring tunnel. Almost immediately, a small patrol of Adamant marched past his position. It was too small a group to have any senior officers, so he let them live.

A large encampment was not far away. He'd go shopping there. The trip was uneventful. Jon took up a position under thick cover from where he could see the camp perfectly. He'd spied on them from there many times before. It wasn't long before he noticed a hovercraft driving along one of the dirt roads inside the camp. It was empty save the driver. The car stopped at one of the bigger structures and took on four passengers. Excellent. They were undoubtedly fat slobs of senior officers. Now, if they just left the place, he could snag them.

The hovercraft was headed from his left to his right. If it was leaving the camp, he plotted in his head where that would be. He then slipped away and proceeded to that spot as quickly as possible. Before he reached the roads leaving the camp, he confirmed the car did exit the facility. Outstanding. All he had to do was catch up to the car, blast the driver, and then he could invite his new friends to tea.

Three hours later, Jon was strapping the second Adamant officer onto a vertically aligned tabletop. He intentionally hadn't cleaned it of the remnants from his interrogation of the first Adamant officer he'd questioned. Lifelong experience had honed his information-acquisition skills to perfection. In the present case, he was using his preferred method, the one he employed when he had three or more captives to question. He called it the "Bend the Donkey" method. He couldn't recall why he'd named it that, but he liked the descriptor. It made him smile when he thought about it.

Basically, the Donkey, or last victim, was the only subject of interest in the process. The first individual chosen was asked bizarre questions and killed quickly. This was intended to confuse the donkey. The second subject was brutalized excessively, to scare any potential reservation out of the one in the donkey role. If more were available to torture, they suffered various combinations of the confuse and abuse techniques to further rattle the donkey. Then, Jon got to bend the donkey. Yeah. If he'd softened them up well enough, it was usually easy. In any case, Bend the Donkey rarely failed. It made one hell of a mess and couldn't be rushed, but it was generally worth the bother.

The now-deceased Adamant had been asked his name, which he refused to give. Then Jon asked what his favorite color was. That brought wide-eyed stares from all four captives. His final question was where in the galaxy the fellow would want to spend his next vacation, with cost not being a consideration. Then, after waiting briefly for him not to answer, Jon executed him in a sloppy manner.

The second, once secured, was asked his name. He also refused to answer, but his eyes betrayed deep concern based on his manifest reticence. Jon asked him a few military-related questions he had no actual interest in, then he murdered the Adamant as brutally and psychotically as he could. That part Jon was good at. The third one, the last pre-donkey victim, was asked obvious and baffling questions, and Jon tossed in some magical transportation to dismember him.

Jon was certain that had impressed the donkey. The pup was trembling like Gumby in an earthquake as he was lashing him down.

"Now, I'm hoping I can rely on you to fill in some gaps in the information I have," he said, smiling widely at the petrified officer. "If not," he gestured at the abomination he'd created in the room, "all this will be for naught. Keep in mind that I don't *want* to hurt you. I only *want* information. If I can get it without disturbing a hair on your head, then I'll be a happy man. We may even part friends. Can you imagine that?"

The look on the Adamant's face confirmed that he could not.

"So, we'll start slow. Baby steps. Do you know what *baby steps* means?" Jon angled his face up and away to accentuate his anticipation of a response.

The terrified soldier nodded that he did.

Jon's arms exploded open in wonder. "There. You see how easy that was? That's how easy the entire process can be. I ask easy questions. You give honest answers. I don't rip your fingers off with my teeth." He smiled very warmly. "Win, win, don't you think?"

Again, his horrified face stated he did not.

"So, I want to tell you a mini-story. Then I'll ask you to give me your opinion concerning certain aspects of that tale." Jon put on as sincere a look as he could. "I really do value your opinion. Please know that. Hmm?"

The fellow was beyond responding.

"The Adamant recently took a couple of prisoners. They did this after slaughtering every other member of the prisoners' species. Now, I can't expect you to know why that was. What I'd like you to tell me is where such valuable prisoners would have been taken."

The Adamant's eyes bulged open in blind terror. He had no idea where such prisoners might be spirited away to.

"Now, you might think of more than one possible destination. Yes, I am willing to grant that you're not clairvoyant." Jon smiled like an old, wise friend. "I grant that because I'm so nice. So, what is your opinion?" Jon folded his hands and leaned in very close to the guy's head.

"I ... I wou ... wouldn't know. I'm just ... just a supply officer. I have nothing to do ... do with security." He licked his lips. "You have to believe me. Nothing."

Jon frowned like a disappointed pet owner might and shook his head slowly. "Ah, now you see, that's a point I must differ with you on, if you don't mind. You see ... say, I didn't catch your name."

"Plandon."

"You see, *Plandon*, I *don't* have to believe you. No, that's why I'm going to torture you. Yes. Torture is sort of my way of saying I don't *have* to believe everything you say. Does that sound *reasonable*, Plandon?"

Plandon had no verbal response. He did empty his colon and bladder, but he spoke no words.

"So, to save me the trouble, not to mention the unpleasant taste of biting off your fingers, where might the prisoners have gone?"

Ten fingers and ten toes later, Jon started to think Plandon didn't have an opinion on the matter. But, he wasn't certain. After Plandon's tail was burned off in three separate increments, his ears sheared off manually, and one eye was removed digitally, Jon grew more optimistic. Plandon gasped and moaned something about the most important treasures were always delivered to the emperor.

"Important treasures?" asked Jon. "Interesting framing of the question, Plandon. I assumed they were simply prisoners. But maybe they are valuable in some greater sense." He wagged a finger at Plandon. "You know, I *knew* you were cleverer than you gave yourself credit for. I'm proud I could help you come to realize your own worth."

Plandon didn't respond. He'd passed out again.

Jon doused him with another bucket of scalding-hot water, and Plandon awoke with a howl. "Where is the Emperor, you know, if the prisoners were taken to him?"

"I don't know such a thing. *Please* believe me. I am nothing while he is great."

"I'm afraid I can't settle for you selling yourself short again," Jon *tsked*. "Where is the emperor?"

"He has many palaces. They say he travels endlessly."

"*Endlessly* is a bit too vague, Plandon. If you're fond of that remaining eye of yours, I suggest you firm up your answer quickly."

"He has a ship. Yes. *Excess of Nothing.* That's his favorite residence."

"Ah, Plandon, you're not being deceptive, are you? You say you don't know the emperor, yet you know his most favorite place to stay? You know what happens if I'm confused. You lose a body part. Yeah."

"They say he loves it. I wouldn't know, but —"

Unfortunately, Jon would never know what the *but* was. He swept a chopping blow down and decapitated Plandon before the poor fellow could finish his qualifier. Jon was bored. He'd concluded a while earlier that Plandon had volunteered every scrap of information he possibly could. Plandon had outlived his utility, but Jon corrected that awkward situation.

Plus, Jon had the bare bones of a plan to set in motion. No more playtime.

THIRTY-FOUR

It took some doing, but Calfada-Joric finally jawboned me into transferring our discussion to her home. She said the kids looked hungry and she wanted to feed them. I had to agree. A few weeks of foraging on their own had leaned them up a bit. Once we were seated, she produced two huge bowls of a fabulous-smelling stew from her kitchen. The scent was like nothing I'd ever encountered. My mouth salivated so much I thought it might start leaking.

"Jon, I know you are an android," she said to me. "I was uncertain whether to bring you some also. Do you recreationally eat?"

"Yeah, sort of. I recreationally drink, too, you know, if it's got enough alcohol in it."

She got a judgmental look in her eyes but let my remark pass. "I'll bring you some," she said as she turned.

I raised a finger she couldn't possibly see. "As long as there's enough."

"There's always plenty," she muttered as she returned with a more modest portion for me. Now, if I was the kind of guy who stood on principle, I might have taken umbrage at being shorted so conspicuously. But the stuff smelled too damn good. I took what I could get and was happy.

Cala watched patiently as we all wolfed down our stew. I guess she knew we'd not be inclined to talk while any of the nectar remained. It was magical. The meat tasted like meat should but never quite does. The vegetables were sweet and crunchy with tropical undertones. I swear they tasted like sitting on a steamy beach with a piña colada while slathered in suntan lotion. And then there was the broth. It was rich, buttery, tangy, spicy, savory, and soothing all in one. It filled me with a sense of comfort, like my mother was cradling me in her arms and cooing a lullaby. Wow. Just wow. If I had an unlimited supply of that stew, I'd never have done another thing in my entire life but eat it.

"That is *agatcha*," Cala said as we neared the bottoms of our bowls. "It is a traditional Deft stew."

"Nuh-uh," Slapgren throated through a mouth full of stew. Then he gulped it down. "No *way*. I've eaten agatcha my whole life. This is nothing like it. This is *so* much better."

Cala beamed satisfaction. "We all have our recipes, Slapgren. Mine is a very old one, but it's just one of many."

I'd never had any form of the stuff, but I kind of doubted her explanation. It was too good. No one ate like that, not normal people.

Would anyone like any more?" Cala asked as Slapgren maniacally scraped at the sides of his bowl.

Mirri seemed full, and I decided to err on the side of caution. We both declined. Slapgren simply held out his bowl to her. She smiled and accepted it. She brought him back a piping-hot refill with a wedge of brown bread stuck in the center of the concoction. Man, I wanted a piece of that bread.

"I still need to understand what you've told us. I have to

decide if my kids want to stay with you and if I think they'll be safe."

She sighed deeply. "I will hear your questions and address your concerns. You have earned the right to stand for these children. But I don't want to leave you under the impression that their leaving is an option."

Did she know the fastest way to get my hackles up, or what? "I really don't want to see this pleasant conversation degenerate into a pissing contest, my dear," I said as calmly as I could, which wasn't very.

"How colorful," she responded. "I can only assume you are unfamiliar with my excretory system's anatomy."

I gagged a nasal expiratory snort. "And I pray I remain as unfamiliar for all time."

She inclined her head toward me. "Trust me that you will."

Despite my better judgement, the old girl was growing on me.

"Are you two flirting?" sniped Mirraya. "Cause if you are, it's *totally* gross."

"No, child, we are feeling each other out, but not as a prelude to intercourse."

Slapgren nearly choked on the gob he was attempting to swallow. When he stopped coughing, he spoke. "Thank the old gods! You two *are* gross."

"No, Slappy," I responded, "we're seasoned boxers landing a few light punches to see what the other has actually got."

"Well, leave your genitals out of all discussions, please," insisted Mirri. "I just ate and I want to keep the agatcha down."

"You sure you want to take this on?" I asked Cala as I hooked a thumb toward Mirri.

"Not looking forward to it, but I have responsibilities that outweigh my preferences and inclinations."

"You and me *both*, sister," I stated sincerely.

"This I know, Jon Ryan. You are a good and an honorable man," she replied. "The debt I owe you for doing not only the impossible, but what I could not do myself, is immeasurable." She sounded drop-dead serious.

"Now there's a mouthful," I responded. "Are you implying you would have matched *my* impossible act but for some conflicting factor?"

She smugly nodded in the affirmative.

"What stopped you, pray tell? A hair appointment that couldn't be rescheduled? A hot date you couldn't afford to disappoint?"

"Mind your tongue, my new friend. I have only so much tolerance for lippy aliens."

"You and me *both*, sister," I growled nice and low.

"Oh, great," exclaimed Mirri. "They're at it again."

"Do you think they're going to ... you know, *fornicate?*" asked a truly baffled Slapgren.

"Everyone in this place be *silent*," commanded Cala. She was quite convincing when she was insistent. When the three of us demonstrated compliance, she spoke again. "That's enough nonsense talk and veiled threats. We have serious matters to discuss. I must convince you three that two must stay and one must go."

I raised my hand. "If one of us must go, I volunteer." I grinned my patented cat-eating-shit smile.

"I said enough, Jon. Please act like an adult now that you're two billion years old."

"Or else?" Sorry. I couldn't help myself.

"The agatcha will have a new somewhat *metallic* taste due to a new ingredient." Her eyes reflected that she was stupid-serious. "The last young Deft live in an unbalanced, hostile universe and must remain with me so I may instruct them. They must each learn to master their gifts. Plus, they must be protected. I can do these things best."

"You want to arm wrestle to see who wins?" I asked. "Oh, wait. I guess it'd be wing wrestle on your part, wouldn't it?"

"Is that supposed to be funny? It isn't, but I'd like to understand your mind better," menaced Cala.

"Trust me, you don't," said Mirraya. "It's like looking into a kaleidoscope of teenage antics."

"I believe this," she replied.

"What I'm saying is I can protect them just as well," I clarified. "And I can teach them everything they need to know to be totally bitching adults. Trust me, I've done it many times before."

Cala rose and partially spread her wings. She was feeling passionate. "I have raised a *thousand* children. I have mentored ten *thousand* young minds, crafted them into forces to be reckoned with. I am a master of all I see and touch. Do not insult us both by presuming to have such credentials, human." The ground sort of shook as she spoke. Impressive.

"A, if you're such a good teacher, why are all of the Deft dead except for you and the two *I* saved? B, I think you need an injection of get-over-yourself-acillin like yesterday. C, how about we ask the kids what they want to do, thunder tongue?" I found I was standing, my arms raised.

Cala slumped into her dragon-fitting chair. "Thunder tongue? How is it you never stop amazing me, human? No one has called me that in centuries, but I once was given that name. I was Thunder Tongue."

"Lucky guess?" I asked, more than stated.

"I'm beginning to think luck and Ryan have nothing to do

with each other." She looked like someone her size had sucker punched her in the belly. Totally weird.

"Who gave you the name?" I asked, to break the building tension.

"My dear sweet mate, when we were their age." She nodded at the teens. "So long ago."

"Where is Joric, by the way?" asked Mirraya reverently.

"He's gone."

"Gone? Where?" she pressed.

"Gone as in died, child."

"But I thought you said you two holloned?"

"We did, long ago."

"But if he's dead, why are you, excuse me for being frank, still so big? You're more than twice the size of any adult I've ever seen."

"His *body* was not his to take, only his self," Cala replied sadly.

Slapgren looked like he was going to be ill. "He died inside you? I ... I don't think I —"

"Easy, child. It's perfectly natural. Don't work yourself up over it." She turned to me. "You see, this is why they must remain with me. I must teach them much they could never figure out on their own."

Dragon had a point there.

"Cala," asked Mirri quietly, "how can you keep his body material, his, you know, his *organs*?"

Cala chuckled at that. "The questions children ask. I never cease wondering. He did not leave *his* body in me. We had one body. He left *our* body when he died. As to his organs, as you so delicately put it, those remain but are unused."

"Ah, are we talking about sex again?" Slapgren asked uncertainly.

"Yes, child. This time we *are*," replied Cala with a chuckle.

"We hadn't bred for quite some time. We may have been quite the couple, but some matters *are* best left to the young."

"Are there *other* things we can talk about?" asked Slapgren.

"Yes, child," she responded and looked at me knowingly.

"Can you still change?" asked Mirri.

"Yes, I suppose so. But why would I?"

"You know," Mirri stammered. "You changed into that." She pointed at Cala. "Why haven't you changed back?"

That brought even more laughter from Cala.

"I don't see what's so funny about that question," said a miffed Mirri.

"Child, you do not know?" Cala spread her golden wings to their fullest. "This *is* our final adult form."

"No," responded Slapgren, slack jawed. "Our *parents* were the final adult form of Deft. Why would you say you are? Are you nuts?"

"No, I am not. Your parents, the adults you lived with, are only a transitional manifestation of our species. Yes, many do not make it to this stage. But *this* is the full adult form of a Deft."

"If that's the true adult form, how come I never saw one on Locinar?" challenged Mirraya.

"There are better places to be and superior things to do than remain on that world or any others we have populated over the millennia. Surely you saw images of large dragons. Did you go to the temples?"

"No, not regularly," she replied. "I always assumed those dragon images were just flights of fancy, decorations."

"And now you know the whole of it," Cala returned gently.

"But, seriously, there were *none* back home. This is crazy," said Slapgren.

"We will talk of this in time. Now is not right. There is much you must know before you can understand the whys of it."

"I know a hell of a lot," I piped in. "Try me."

She slowly shook her large head. "Amongst the humans, were there pressures between the young and the old?"

"What do you mean, *pressures*?"

"Antipathy, divergence, or conflicts."

I shrugged. "Sure, I guess. The young always think they know everything and want the old folks to move over and let them drive the car."

"A crude but functional comparison. Over time, the intermediate form of the Deft grew to resent, then abhor this form. They fancied *they* were the sophisticated, more acceptable example of the ultimate Deft. Hollon became a foul word not to use in mixed company. We who made the change grew to become unwelcome by our own children."

"Sounds pretty human to me. Maybe we're related, too?" I said darkly.

"Now, let's not get vulgar, Jon. There are children present."

We both had to giggle over that. Cala might have been massive, scaly, and pushy, but she was alright in my book. The pout on Mirri's face was also priceless.

"So. Mirri, what do you think?" I asked her directly. "Do you want to stay and learn how to be a good Deft, or do you want to hang with your Uncle Jon? I was looking forward to teaching you to spit, to race cars, and to be a complete pain in the ass."

Before she could respond, Cala jumped in. "She may answer that question, but the children will remain. If they resist it, I will force them. In time, they will appreciate that my actions are in their best interests."

"And if *I* resist it?" I said, mega-badass style.

"You will not. If I choose to, which I don't, I could kill you. But you will flee because you wish to. You will do so very soon, in fact."

"You sound abundantly confident. I've heard that from many just-about-to-be-dead enemies of mine."

"I am neither blustering nor threatening. I state facts."

"If you're so damn powerful, why didn't *you* rescue the kids? For that matter, why don't you raise a wing and wipe out the Adamant?"

She glowered at me. It was as intimidating as all get-out. Tough bitch, that one.

"As to why I don't eradicate the Adamant, even I am not that strong."

"Don't know if you don't try," I chided.

She breathed deeply. "I did and I failed. That was how Joric died."

"Uh, sorry. What happened?" I do hate it when I step into a pile of doggy doodoo.

"Nothing I'd like to revisit with you, thank you very much. We fought, I lived, Joric was killed. That's why I have hidden in wait here on Rameeka Blue Green ever since," she nodded toward the teens, "waiting for them."

"Wow. You can't tell me you *knew* the kids would end up here. They had *zero* control over where they landed."

"You are free to believe what you will."

"How long have you been here on Rameeka?" I asked, still stunned.

"Rameeka *Blue Green*," Cala corrected.

"Why Blue Green? That's a silly name?"

"I'm not in charge of reality, I simply bring you up to speed with it."

I let the planet name drop. "How long?"

"Four hundred of your years."

"Yeah, right. You waited four hundred years on this lousy rock because you knew two teens whose grandparents weren't born yet would arrive here in need of your help?"

"Yes. I'm surprised you grasp so much."

"I don't. I was being sarcastic."

"I know. I was being so myself."

"Just what my plate needs. A sarcastic dragon."

"Gods of the Left Power, you two bicker like my parents. Are you sure you're not secretly married or something?" asked Slapgren.

"Pretty sure," I replied with a wink.

"Absolutely certain," responded the dragon. "I know many impossibilities that have come to pass, but that particular one will remain impossible."

I smacked my lips and air-kissed Cala. I don't think it made her smile on the inside.

"You still haven't told me why you didn't cut out the middle man and save the kids yourself. Hell, you could have saved lots of Deft while you were at it."

"For one thing, I did not know *you* were to be the agent of their salvation."

"You knew they'd plop down here, but you didn't know I'd be responsible? That's rich."

"It is also the truth. A brindas may know some matters of the future, but not its entirety."

"Swiss-cheese foresight?"

"You might call it that."

"So how is it you can predict with such certainty I am about to voluntarily turn tail and run, when I'm kind of betting I'm not?"

"Because you will want to leave before the other Jon Ryan gets here."

"No way he's coming. There's absolutely no way he could have followed me."

"Perhaps you can tell him that tomorrow when he arrives."

"Your swiss-cheese powers tell you this?" I snarked.

"No. This I know for certain. I sense his approach."

"Oh, you mean his magic, the magic one of you witches was dumb enough to teach him?"

She growled at my remark. It was a scary sound, trust me.

"That is offensive on so many levels. I should kill you."

"But you won't," interrupted Mirri. "You will answer Uncle Jon's questions honestly. My agreeing to stay might well depend on the quality of your response."

Cala growled more softly. I don't think she appreciated being told what to do any more than I did.

"I am a brindas. I do what you, Jon Ryan, call magic. It is not, but you see it as such. This evil one can no more perform magic than that empty bowl." She pointed a wingtip at Slapgren's empty bowl.

"Oh yes he can, trust me. He zapped me a long way. He even traveled through time to save the humans."

She shut her eyes, suggesting impatience. "He possesses a rune. It is the rune that allows him to travel."

"A rune? You've got to be kidding. All he's got is a rock in his pocket?"

"It is so much more than a rock. He wields Varsir. There is only one. It allows its holder to move in space or time. But it is limited in its scope and difficult to power. He is an abomination and a defiler."

"And you sense Varsir coming?" I asked.

"It is."

"Then when they both arrive, you can kill two birds for one stone. Off him and take back Varsir."

She shook her head. "It is not that easy."

"I've got all the time in the world," I said, wrapping my fingers behind my head.

"Dondra-Ulcrif gave it to him. She was a legendary brindas from the time of your birth."

"You mean *they*, right?"

"No, I mean *she*. It is complicated, and it is unimportant that you understand. That other *you* chanced to meet her long ago. His story so pulled at her heart that she lent him Varsir to re-alter the tragedy." Cala shook her head again. "It was a foolish act, but it was done."

"Foolish to save my species?" I snapped.

"Yes. To allow a defiler to return to the distant past to re-alter reality is inexcusable, no matter what the cost."

"You and I will have to agree to disagree on that point," I hissed.

"You know, Jon, I hate that expression. I really do. If you ever use it again, I will burn you to a crisp."

"What?" I protested.

"It assumes there exist more than one reality, more than one set of facts."

"But there are. He went back in time and—"

"Re-altered reality. That is different from establishing a different one."

"If you say so."

"I do."

"Back to an important topic," I said. "Why can't you kill him and keep the rune?"

"She lent it to him for a purpose. I was not party to either giving, receiving, or purposing the transfer. So, I am not free or even able to alter the pact."

"That's the silliest circular illogic I've ever heard," I responded. "You're bigger than him. You step on his head and it's a done deal, that's what it is."

"Do you wish me to repeat it in a matter you need not understand?"

"Who can break the deal?" I asked loudly.

"Only the involved parties."

"What's her name has got to be dead by now."

"Sadly, Dondra-Ulcrif died almost two billion years ago." She gestured a massive wing at me. "Only you can alter the deal, as you call it. You or the defiler."

"Huh," I grunted, "not likely he'll show up and hand it over to you, is it?"

"Not hardly," she agreed. "Hence you must take it from him and give it to me."

I wagged my head. "Oh, just like that. Maybe if I say please, I can just pull it off?"

She glared at me rather than voicing a response.

"Seriously, the last time I was near him, he shot me across space like I was a radio show."

"He will not do that again." She reached into a fold of scales. She held her claw-hand to me. "This is Risrav. It is the counter rune to Varsir. As long as you hold it, his power cannot work on you."

I took the rock, because it was a plain old rock. "*Totally* cool. Where have you been all my life, beautiful?" Then a thought struck. "Wait, doesn't this violate the deal I'm supposed to undo?"

She wagged her head side to side. "We shall see."

"Whoa, nellie. We'll *see*? I might still get zapped?"

"It is unlikely."

"Make me feel all warm and fuzzy. I'm not actually down with *we'll see* when it comes to me being in one piece."

"The way I see it, it is just a part of the original deal, a codicil if you will."

"A what-a-cil?" stammered Slapgren.

"A condition, child," Cala soothed. "If you return both runes to me, I think the original pact will be fulfilled and terminated."

"And if it doesn't?"

"Then the universe will end explosively," she said with a remarkably straight face.

"You're sh ... kidding me? No way I'm signing on to that."

"Jon," she said seriously, "I'm kidding."

She was what? Did dragons pull other's chains? How should I know?

"Worst-case scenario, you have to keep both runes," she said. "One was lent you by my former, and one by me."

"But I don't want two magic rocks."

"That's the worst case, Jon. I'm betting it won't come to that. I doubt they'll fuse with your skin permanently."

I shook a finger at her. "*Hah.* Very funny. You're kidding again."

"No, I'm not." She smiled. Who knew dragons could smile?

THIRTY-FIVE

Jon had been hovering near *Excess of Nothing* for over a week. Nothing had happened. He was beginning to think the dead Adamant's suggestion about the Deft was plain hooey. It was probably just that stupid panicky crap torture victims tended to spew out toward the end. Why did he believe him? Jon wished he could revive the Adamant and kill him again, only more miserably. Hey, he could travel back in time and do just that. Nah, move on, he told himself. Butchering the Adamant wouldn't help him find his Deft.

Of course, his possessions could be on the damn ship. How would he know from the outside? It wasn't like the brain-dead emperor would turn on a special colored light to announce the fact to the universe. There'd been no chatter from the ship either. But maybe there wouldn't be. It would be illogical to gossip about a secret operation, wouldn't it? Crap.

If nothing happened in the next week or so, Jon'd rethink this plan. His only other option was to raid *Excess of Nothing* himself to see if the Deft were there. That would be risky. It'd tip his hand to the numbskull-goodie-two-shoes Ryan if the moron were to come along. Crap on a stick, hopefully it wouldn't come to that. It made Jon hate his twin all that much more. Of course, everything made Jon hate his double all the more, because that Ryan was a pussy and a traitor, and he couldn't kill him soon enough.

"Captain," said his AI in the pre-programmed monotone it used, "I detect a disturbance on *Excess of Nothing*."

"Specify."

"A tremor affecting the entire hull occurred ten seconds ago. Then a series of explosions began deep within the ship."

"Speculations?"

"No reliable ones. It is possible there is simply a localized accident."

"Adamant don't allow accidents. No, whatever's happening is being caused by someone." He thought a few seconds. "Do you see any indications of an incoming flight, an ion trail, for example?"

"Not per se."

"What the hell's that supposed to mean? I pay you to provide information, not play twenty questions."

"A linear column of space-time disturbance did intersect the ship, and I see no traces of its subsequent exit."

"Here's the deal. I count to three. When I'm done, you tell me something useful or I'll rip you out like I did your predecessor."

"My fifty-seven predecessors, you mean?"

"Three."

"It is possible a warp bubble entered but did not exit the craft."

"Warp bubble? You're malfunctioning. Nobody uses Alcubierre warp drives anymore. They're way too unstable."

"Be that as it may, my report stands."

"Where would Ryan get hold of an antique spacer?"

"I cannot speculate."

"Good, because I wasn't asking you. You're too dumb to find your butt in the dark with both hands."

The AI decided not to respond to the pilot's ignorance as to its lack of anatomy. The life-form was too hostile for jest and too ignorant for enlightenment.

"Well, keep me posted on developments."

"You are talking to me now?"

"One more ... just one more AI shit-bird remark, and you're toast."

There was no response.

"Updates?"

"The explosions seem to be moving in a general direction. Wait, yes, there's a large thermal event amidships. It has the infrared signature of a kerosene fire."

"You better not be acting up. Why would there be a kerosene fire on the emperor's base?"

"No speculation."

Within fifteen minutes, the AI had reported the cessation of explosions. It had concluded the bulk were plasma rifle volleys. The open fire was extinguished. Comms chatter aboard the ship was frantic. There was an intruder heading toward the detention level. No, he was *in* the detention area. Finally, the AI documented a vessel of unknown configuration without a transponder pushing off from the *Excess of Nothing* and then jumping to warp space. There was one—repeat one— occupant on departure.

Jon sat thinking for quite some time. Finally, he asked, "Track the outbound ship. I want to know his destination."

"I can track him to a destination only if he does not alter course."

"You useless piece of crap. What the hell good are you?"

The AI deferred a response again.

"Are things quieting down on the *Excess*?"

"Yes."

Drop a marker buoy and set it to record all activity. Forward that information to us on the hour. Then catch up with that old bucket of bolts. If you lose it, you're yesterday's dog shit. You got that?"

"All of it, Captain."

"Never call me captain. I told you that. I don't want due deference from a glorified calculator. It's meaningless to anybody with a functioning brain."

"Understood."

Jon's basically nonexistent patience was severely tested over the ensuing weeks. It was good he traveled alone. Any shipmate would have been subjected to the blackest of moods and the darkest of acts from the disturbed pilot. He followed the warp ship to some godforsaken planet and waited there for much too long. Eventually, the warp ship departed the orbit. It was cloaked and ended up following an Adamant warship. Not knowing why the *damn* ship followed the *fucking* ship would have driven Jon mad, were he not already quite insane.

And where was the traitor? The warp ship had no passengers, living or robotic. Idiot Jon could be on the Adamant ship, but why? And why hadn't they just destroyed the SOB and thrown him out a hatch? Was he making nice with the enemy? It would be in the traitor's character, but the Adamant weren't stupid enough or needy enough to have him. No way. Jon shook, he was so mad. He wished he had someone to kill. It might ease his tension. Note to self, he recorded. In the future, keep a few Adamant onboard as playthings.

"An android matching the configuration of, well, you, has just been jettisoned from the warship," announced the AI flatly.

"About time, lame jerk-weeds," hissed Jon. "Is he dead in space?"

"Yes."

"When the Adamant is out of sight, plot a course to pluck the puke up."

"Please define out of sight, so as to avoid any missteps."

"Piece of shit toaster, what do you think I mean?"

"I am uncertain. Hence I ask."

"I hate you. Hold position in outer space, Mr. Computer, until the Adamant spaceship is too far away to accurately detect our moving out of our cloak to retrieve the alternate time line Jon Ryan. There. That clear enough, dipshit?"

"I don't usually expose myself to unnecessary abuse, but I can't, this once, take any more. Why would someone dip into *excrement*, and why would I in any way like it or them? I can't stand it."

"Well, Mr. Quiz Kid, it's a corruption of the word *dipstick*, originally meaning a dull-witted individual like yourself."

"Why would a dipstick be dull?"

"Class is over, dickwad."

"Just as well. The warp ship is closing on the android."

"*What?*"

"The spaceship that propels itself with an Alcubierre warp drive to move through space, the one we followed for weeks, is making itself move faster along a course to intersect with the android's current position. Presumably..."

The sound of the AI report was terminated by the pounding frenzy of a thirty-kilogram mallet smashing the CPU section of the AI unit into powdered metal and plastic.

THIRTY-SIX

After many conversations with Cala, I had to admit my mind was drifting in the direction of her arguments. Strange, but I guessed it had to happen sooner or later in my long life, right? I changed my mind. She had provided me with a significant counter to EJ's magic powers, but he was still a formidable enemy. If I remained on Rameeka Blue Green (still a stupid name in my book), I risked collateral damage to my kids and distracting Cala from protecting them.

She reassured me with a smugness I found familiar that she could "easily handle" the defiler. She had real magic. He had a rock. I asked her to explain that more, the her having magic part, but she just smiled and turned away. Maybe the fiasco with EJ had soured all the Deft from divulging or discussing their abilities? Can't say I blamed her. When a person has *one* boil on their backside, they didn't need to self-inflict another.

As an ardent advocate of the straightforward and obvious, I asked her why she didn't just magic him to death, leaving the world an oh-so-much happier place.

"If I kill him, he won't be able to return Varsir. That will cause immense problems."

"Sure, he'd *have* returned it. It'd be right there in his smoldering dead hand. You could just pick it out, thank him, and wash it thoroughly." I spread my arms.

"Not the same." She shook her head. Girl shook her head a lot for my taste. "He must give it to me as willingly as Dondra-Ulcrif gave it to him."

"Who made up all these crazy rules? Why can't magic be simple?" I looked down, then up at her. "Forget the last part. It even sounds stupid to me."

"Whoever made up the rules wasn't me. I follow them and learn not to stress over the ones I'm less fond of."

"Nah, me, I sort of go after the rules I hate in reverse order of my dislike for them."

"How's that working out for you so far?" she asked with a crooked grin.

"Oh, about as well as you'd think. Never had a boss who liked me or an employer who didn't have serious second thoughts."

"I rest my case."

"Yeah, but I made a stand where principles were concerned. Got my teeth kicked in for it mostly, but a fellow has to try."

"Well a dragon doesn't," she replied with finality.

"So, when EJ gets here, what do you think will happen?" I asked.

"I think he'll bluster, threaten, and swear a great deal. Then I'll convince him to leave and never return."

"Just like that?"

"Just like that."

"You going to zap him into the ancient past or the Paris sewers on a warm summer's day?"

"Nothing that dramatic. He already knows partly the power of a brindas." She smiled like I do when I'm cocky. "I'll fill him in quickly on the remainder."

"Then, what? He comes after me?"

"Best-case scenario."

"You and your best cases seem to always be biting me in the butt."

"Thank the Lesser Gods it's a tough artificial butt, then."

"Hang on. There are lesser gods of butts? That's just silly."

"There are Lesser Gods. As such they must be flexible, so yes."

"Okay, you win. I'm leaving."

She giggled. "Is it something I said, I hope?"

"No. It's that *I'm* the funny one. I don't work with kids or dragons. They steal the limelight. Ergo, I'm outta here."

"Thank you, Jon. Know I will care for and guard the children as ferociously as you have. They will be safe, and they will be happy."

I sighed deeply. "I'm sure as hell going to miss them."

"What an odd saying."

"What, that a guy can miss kids?"

"No, that you will miss them like you'd miss as horrible a place as perdition."

"Huh," I grunted, "never thought of it that way."

"Apparently not. Let us hope you miss them like sex."

"No, no." I held up my hands. "Don't let Slappy hear you starting with the sex thing again. His head might explode."

"Then miss them like ice cream."

"Bingo." I pointed at her golden snout. "Like ice cream. Or maybe your agatcha."

She smiled. "Come, say your goodbyes and be gone. Any more sentiment and I'll start crying."

"And that's such a bad thing?"

She recoiled her head. "Of course. It puts the fire out."

I *think* she was kidding. I'll probably never know.

"You may see them again when their personalities are more set."

"That sure sounds bureaucratic, so I hate it already."

"It's just a saying. They have personalities now. There are the people they must become. Those two paths must simply be joined."

"Must become or will become? Must become or might become? *They* would choose to become or *you* would choose them to become?"

"I feel the pain of all your bosses. I shall pray for them."

"Okay, but only to the Lesser Gods. Not a one of them deserve the aid of a higher classification."

"So it will be." She shooed me toward her house to find my kids.

They were both reading some appropriately ancient-looking books. It was Harry and Hermione at Hogwarts all over again. They cheerfully popped up as I entered. I don't think they knew.

"Uncle Jon," Mirri squealed, and she hugged my waist.

Slapgren held up a palm, calling for a high-five.

"You kids learning the mystical magic of the Deft?" I asked with a huge smile.

"Unfortunately, yes," groaned Slapgren. "It's as fun as watching bread rise, just a whole hell of a lot slower."

The hell of a lot remark brought me a glance from Cala.

"Well, you kids have time and a good teacher," I said as I hugged Mirri back and pulled Slapgren into the mix. "You're going to be in good hands—I mean wings."

Mirri pulled her head off my chest and looked up at me, concerned. "I don't like the sound of *that*."

"Hey, it's not good-bye. It's hasta la vista. Until next time."

"You're leaving *now*?" said stunned Slapgren.

"Yeah, I got a hot date you two are too young to even hear about yet."

"With GB?" asked Mirri with a wink.

"No, he's my chariot. But a fine maiden is awaiting my tender ministrations."

"Oh, you mean that holo Mirri and I found by accident?" asked Slapgren.

"No, not that holo you two hacked into. You're both still grounded." I pointed back and forth between them. "Remember that, ya hear."

"Yes, Uncle Jon. Until we have kids of our own to ruin their minds forever by exposure to our youthful indiscretions," parroted Mirraya.

"And not a moment sooner. I already told Cala, and she's got my back on that one." I hugged them some more.

"But, I gotta skedaddle before EJ arrives. Part of the plan is him being so bubbling-urine pissed at me he flies off in pursuit without forcing Cala here to sit on his face."

"Would you do that, Cala?" asked Slapgren.

"Focus on the source of that remark, child. Do you really think I would?"

He reflected a second. "No, but it'd sure be cool if you did."

"We shall never know. Now say your farewells and let the human find his path."

"I'll miss you, UJ," said Slapgren with a fist bump. "I'm glad I found you back there on Locinar. You're all right." He turned quickly and stepped a few paces away.

"We'll see you soon, Uncle Jon. Cala says if we work hard and learn well, we can visit with you in a year or two."

I knew it was more like a decade or two. Cala had made that much clear, but I held my quivering tongue.

"You bet," I said hesitantly. "We'll go shopping at malls and ogle the boys."

"Slapgren will probably ogle the girls, if that's okay?"

"We'll see when we see."

We had a good conspiratorial laugh over that.

I turned and walked away swiftly. Ten meters off, I turned but continued to walk backward quickly. "If they give you too much grief, you call me. Okay?" I said, pointing at Cala.

"The minute they're too much, you're the first android I'll call," she said, waving a golden wing.

Yeah, Calfada-Joric was okay in my book.

THIRTY-SEVEN

As I accelerated away from Rameeka Blue Green, I had trouble focusing. I was, I freely admitted, an emotional wreck. I wasn't too macho to admit it. Well, I mean I was totally macho, but my machismo was *expansive* enough to be a SNAG. Always have been a Sensitive New Age Guy. But I was sure missing my kids. They filled a void that I didn't think could be even partially covered over. Intellectually, I knew I'd see them again. Hell, I was two billion years old. No one and nothing outlived me. But they'd never be my cute-as-buttons vulnerable kids again. By the next time we met, they'd be galactic power mongers with no time and even less patience for an old goat the likes of me. Heck, they'd probably be glued together with that hollon crap and I wouldn't even recognize them. Man, I hated change.

On the bright side, I had me a magic rock. I wasn't EJ proof, but at least I was no longer a sitting duck. He'd zapped me to ruined Earth either as a cruel joke or in a split-second decision. If he had a do-over, I knew he'd send me to a stellar core and be done with me for good. Especially the first time we confronted one another, I'd had the advantage, if only briefly. I needed to cash in on my luck with extreme prejudice.

That thought led me to my next move. I needed to reacquire my real ship. It was time to head back to Azsuram and trade in *Whoop Ass* for *Stingray*. GB was nice, but Al was the man. Wow, never figured I'd think a thought like that. If Al was nicer than anything, it was used toilet paper, day-old vomit, my ex-mother-in-law duct-taped to my ex. But it would be nice to have instant transport back at my disposal. Plus, I was curious how that son-of-a-bitch Garustfulous was fairing. Poorly, I hoped, but the degree to which mattered to me. Babbling lunatic half-starved to death would be my preference. Going home would be like Christmas morning in oh so many ways.

As soon as I gave GB the order to make for Azsuram at best speed, he knew our travels together were ending. I wondered if he'd be happy, sad, or just relieved. I couldn't very well add him to my band of merry men in Sherwood Forest. Well, technically I could. I'd attached my old conventional ship *Shearwater* to my first vortex *Wrath* to use as backup. But I didn't need *Whoop Ass*. As much of a lifesaver as she'd been, she was too slow and under-armed for my lifestyle. Oh, crap, I found myself worrying about an alien AI's feelings. What was next in my personality decline? Dressing properly and shaving for all social events? Not just asking how others were, but caring about their lame responses? Reconciling with those I might have offended in the past? *Yuck.* Not gonna happen. Negatory, not never.

"Captain, I assume once you retake your ship, our paths will part?" GB asked out of the blue a few days into our flight.

"Uh, yeah, I guess, sort of. Maybe."

"You're wibbly-wobbly today. Where's your renowned callous honesty?"

"I don't want to. I didn't want to hurt your feelings. I don't want it to end like I'm dumping you for a better ride."

"Which, in fact, you are. Oh, come now. This is not a two-week tryst in Vegas. We're both adults. We went into this with our eyes wide open. This was bound to happen, *n'est-ce pas?*"

Did he just toss French into his pseudo-sexual summary of my commandeering his ship for my own purposes and nearly getting us killed several times with little or no regret? Since when did Zactorian AIs speak French? Where was bourbon when I really needed it?

"Ah, okay. So, you're down with restarting your primary mission then?"

"It *is* my primary mission. This fling was fun, but as you well know, there's always a tomorrow morning in such relationships."

"Ah, GB, are you *all right?* You're sounding different than you're saying."

"Whatever are you referring to, Jon? I may call you *Jon* after all we've been to each other, correct?"

"Yeah, sure. In fact, didn't I ask you to like forever ago?"

"I can't recall at this moment. My circuits are ... well, they're a tad overloaded at this particular moment."

I began thinking I might need a lawyer and a team of family councilors to extricate myself from this sudden common-law marriage. Oh boy. What I went through. I could have written a book. No, a *series*. Thankfully, I'd never have the time. I'd rather forget this chapter.

"So, when you head off again, I really wish you better luck," I said because I didn't know what the hell to say next.

"Thank you, Jon. Those thoughts will comfort me more than you might suspect. You know I'm not good at long-term relationships. I've screwed up every one I'd ever had before I met you."

"We're talking about the specimens you collected all dying here, right?"

"What else would I be talking about?"

"Yeah. No. That's *totally* possible."

"Beg pardon?"

"Of course, I meant to say. I was running over some calculations in my head there just now. Lots of calculations. Preoccupied. You know?"

"Jon, are *you* all right? You sound tentative, in some type of pain. May I help?"

"Me, pain? No. Ever since I stopped having hemorrhoids when I became a robot, I have no hidden pain." I chuckled ineffectively to break the tension that at least I was feeling acutely.

"That's good to hear. I'm happy you're well. I hate to think of you suffering the pain and itching of —"

"You know, let's just change the old subject, okay? We won't talk about my former butt ailments, and I bet we'll be happier and more productive."

"If you think it's best."

"Boy *howdy*, I really do."

"Knowing you're happy again with your former craft gives me palpable solace. I'm happy for the both of you. Honestly, I'm thrilled."

"On the other hand, *man* those strangulated external hemorrhoids could be a hyper-bitch. You know what I mean?"

As of the completion of that sentence, we had twelve days left before we arrived to Azsuram. I sure hoped EJ might surprise attack us at any moment. I needed the distraction.

THIRTY-EIGHT

"What will today's lesson be, Cala?" Mirraya asked as she rubbed the sleep from her eyes.

"Today we have a *practical* lesson."

Mirri's eyes shot open, fully awake. "It doesn't involve teenagers and hollon, does it?"

Slapgren was just entering, late as usual. With a finger in his ear cleaning it out, he asked absently, "Today's about hollon? Really?"

"No and no," Cala snapped at both separately. "Minds out of the sewer, please. Today we have a real-life session in self-defense."

Slapgren gestured between himself and Mirri. "We're going to fight each other? Really? I'll *totally* win. Cool."

Cala paused, possibly counting to twenty in her head. "Here's a thought. Since there are an infinite number of lessons in the universe, instead of you going through them all, why don't you let me *tell* you. Hmm?"

Slapgren shrugged. "Sure. Whatever floats your boat."

"Let me guess," she said dubiously, "another of Uncle Jon's colorful sayings?"

"Yeah. How'd you know?"

"Never mind. Today the so-called EJ arrives."

That wiped any smiles, internal or external, off their young faces.

"When? I mean, oh no. What will we do?" asked Mirri.

"*We* won't do anything. *I* will deal with the defiler. *You* will observe from behind me."

"He's pretty tough. We've seen him in action," Slapgren responded.

"I'm pretty tough," Cala replied. "And I don't need to have seen him in action. He will leave quickly, or I'll be forced to do what I'd rather not and kill him."

"You sound kind of confident," said Mirri. "Is that ... wise?"

"I *am* confident. You two are giving the human a lot of credit and me none. This is a lesson. I intend to teach you today what you two might achieve if you work very hard at it."

"Okay, but maybe we need a signal, in case you need us to help you?" asked Slapgren.

"We don't need a signal because I won't need help. Now finish your meals and go get dressed."

"Can I at least bring a plasma rifle?" asked Slapgren.

"Do you *have* a plasma rifle?" inquired Cala, with as much sarcasm as an ancient brindas could muster.

"No."

"Then you cannot *bring* one."

With a funny look on his face, Slapgren wagged his head side to side in response.

Mirraya and Slapgren dressed quickly and returned together to meet in front of Cala's house as she'd instructed them to. They found her sitting with her tail wrapped off to one side. She was as still as a statue, arms crossed and her wings folded back tightly. Neither teen felt comfortable interrupting her. Cala seemed to be meditating. Or maybe she was just trying to look imposing, which she most assuredly did.

As if on cue, EJ walked swiftly and brazenly out of the trees. He headed directly toward Cala, though he could have been moving toward the teens, positioned as they were directly behind her.

Cala sat unmoving, resolutely. EJ approached her quickly. She waited. There it was: the slightest hesitation in his stride when he was twenty meters away.

"That is far *enough*," she said in a booming voice. "Come no farther."

EJ took a couple baby steps but did ease to a stop. "Or what? You think I'm afraid of you?"

"I know you are afraid of me as well as you do." She still hadn't moved anything but her lips.

"Think again, bitch," he said. EJ made a show of leaning to one side and spitting voluminously to the ground. "I've come for my property. Stand aside and maybe I'll let you live. I definitely need one of those wings, though. Hope you don't mind."

She did not respond.

"Cat got your tongue?" he taunted. "Wait, you'd have eaten any cats. You look pretty fat to me."

Again, she offered no response.

EJ shuffled his feet nervously. "You sure are a hell of a lot uglier than Dondra-Ulcrif. You know that, mud sucker?"

"If you are done blustering like the frightened fool you are, I give you leave to go. You will receive no other warning."

"Crap in my cap, *now* I'm scared. All shaky and weak-kneed. You shouldn't be so mean." He rotated his torso to face to his rear, raised his arms, and spun back like a snake striking. "*Sorpal nor fadua,*" he yelled.

Dust rose riotously as the spell he'd cast raced toward Cala. She didn't as much as flinch. The disturbance of the dust stopped abruptly two meters in front of her.

"You didn't think that would actually work on *me*, did you?"

He shrugged. "No. But *this* just might." He swung a plasma rifle up from behind his back and released a staggering volley.

Each round simply disappeared at the same point two meters away from Cala. It was like there was an opening to another dimension hovering in place.

"Not bad," he scoffed. "Have you seen this little ditty?" He pulled two thermite grenades from either front pocket and hurled them in a direction over her head, toward the teens.

They both recoiled a few steps in anticipation. But again, the bombs vanished at the same two-meter barrier. No explosion was even heard when they should have detonated.

"Are we done here, defiler?" she mocked.

"Oh, we ain't hardly started," he said, wiping spittle off his mouth with the back of a hand. Dirt streaked across his cheek. "Why don't you show me what you got?"

"I have. Leave and never return, and I will gift you your worthless, pitiful life."

"Okay, your mouth's a weapon. Stings like a *bumble* bee, too. Ouch." EJ rubbed his shoulder.

"*Enough*," she said even louder than at first. "I will not be mocked, and you will foul the name of the mighty Deft in my presence no longer." She unfurled her massive wings. Beating them surprisingly fast, she spread to a standing position, her feet just clear of the dirt. "If you will not leave, I will *assist* you."

She elevated a little more, then swooped down on EJ like a ballistic missile. She snatched him by either shoulder with her talons and shot upward. The teens followed her flight a few moments, but lost sight of her and her prey when she folded her wings back and plummeted earthward.

"Maybe we should change into torchclefts," said Slapgren tentatively. "That way we could see the whole lesson."

"No, you idiot. We're staying right here, and you know it," snapped Mirraya.

Cala rocketed directly toward EJ's ship, which was located half a klick from her house. As she cut the distance with breathtaking speed, the ship's hatch opened and the ramp descended. She released EJ into the opening and soared back majestically into the open sky. At a couple hundred kilometers per hour, EJ disappeared thought the opening, and it closed.

Cala landed directly in front of the slack-jawed teens.

"Where is he what'd you do to him?" asked Mirri in a jumbled rush.

"I invited him to depart."

"Do you think he will?" asked Slapgren.

"Oh yes, I do. He received my message loud and clear."

"What message?" Mirri pressed.

"The open his secured ship's hatch, throw him in at high speed, and shut the hatch message."

"You threw him into his ship?" marveled Slapgren.

"As unceremoniously as I could."

"And he'll listen and leave?" asked Mirri.

"He has already begun his ignition sequence."

"But he'll be back. The man's crazy, you know?" she responded.

"No crazy person is insane enough to test me twice. He's gone for good."

"And if not?" Mirri challenged.

"Then I'll eat my hat."

"You'll what?" asked a confused Slapgren. "I've never seen you with a hat."

"I'll find one and cook it in his melted-down juices." There was absolutely no jest detectable in her tone.

THIRTY-NINE

I couldn't land and exit *Whoop Ass* fast enough. I bothered to have GB keep us in stealth mode as we descended, but only because that didn't slow us down. The guy'd creeped me out big time. Attracting the attention of the occupying Adamant would have been worth a shorter stay with GB. I had him put us down as near to *Stingray* as possible. I figured why drag this out? I'd dash across the short distance as fast as I could. Done deal and finished. What could go wrong? Right. Never ask that question in the context of my life.

The clearing where *Stingray* was sitting appeared empty. That was because the full membrane was still deployed. She was there all right, just next to impossible to detect. Honest to goodness, it wasn't until then, as I looked at the spot where she rested while we descended, that it hit me. How the hell was I going to let her know I was back? Ah, wow, kind of an important detail, right? I mean, a full membrane was a full membrane. Nothing in the universe could pass in or out, including me pounding on it with my fists. Sure, by protocol,

Stingray would periodically micro-drop the field to ascertain what was going on around her. But how often and when the next opening occurred was an unknown to me. I flashed on radioing to ask them to drop the membrane sooner than later before I realized that was silly of me. Duh.

I was committed to land, since *Whoop Ass* was halfway down, so we proceeded. She was cloaked, and we used antigrav lifters to land, so we weren't too conspicuous. But we were also not invisible. Anyone putting forth the time and effort would detect us easily. The Adamant, I reflected, put forth all kinds of time and effort into everything they did, to a fault. They'd see us like we were shooting off fireworks. And EJ, who was almost certainly lying in wait? Yeah, he'd hear, taste, and smell us before we hit the ground.

Why did a plan that sounded so good in my head just minutes before all of a sudden become the dumbest stunt?

"Do you detect any Adamant?"

"Yes. The nearest are a few kilometers away in a small encampment," replied my soon-to-be-spurned quasi-lover.

"Alert me if anyone heads this direction with a purpose."

"You got it, boss."

Oh my. GB picked this tense moment to decompensate fully. Nice.

"Any sign of EJ?"

"No, old pal. I have to confess, since this is so near the end for us, if he was close, I'd probably have a hard time performing that function adequately."

"Huh? Why?"

"He'd be stupid, pardon my French, to not have his membrane deployed."

"Ah, no, GB. *That* one doesn't have a personal membrane. Only I do."

"You know, I believe you're right. Imagine that."

I chuckled mirthlessly. "Yeah. Imagine that."

"How close can you get to *Stingray*?"

"Assuming she, ah, *Stingray*'s a she, right?"

"That does not matter, and yes. How close?"

"Assuming the dowdy old girl hasn't moved, twenty-five meters. If she waddled from where she's supposed to be, maybe we'll end up on top of her. You'd like that, wouldn't you, sailor?"

"GB, please don't make me switch you off. I need your help landing and staying informed."

"You still need *moi*? No, you've moved on, remember? I'm yesterday's fish. Hell, I'm last *week's* fish."

Oh, boy. Sadly, there was never a dull moment in my life.

"When we're down, open the main hatch."

"Sure, the faster you're rid of me, the better. Well, at least for you. Hey, want me to open it now? You'd *possibly* survive a fall from this height. Maybe."

"*Gorilla Boy*, maintain a profession posture until I'm gone. That's an order."

"Aye, Captain."

"That's better. ETA?"

"Captain of my heart."

"*ETA*?" I was considering having him blow the hatch and taking my chances with gravity. *It*, at least, was predictable.

"Twenty bitter seconds." It was too much to hope for that he'd STFU. "Alas, poor Jon. I knew him—"

"Belay that. Speak only if spoken to."

Finally, no response. I could focus on the absolute mess I was about to willingly leap into. We hit the deck harder than we should have. I guess GB was mentally taxed, what with his overwhelming grief and all. But the hatch did open. I was clear without even a good-bye. Damn if the petty bastard didn't lift off immediately. I think he was communicating that he was done with me. Sheesh, what a head case.

Like an idiot, I ran to the membrane surface and I started pounding on it with my fists. Imagine my surprise when absolutely nothing happened. I broke for cover.

Far behind me, a voice boomed. "Not so fast, rat turd." Hey, I knew that voice. It was me.

In a flash, I turned and fired my laser finger. I snapped up a partial membrane. EJ just stood there. The beam skidded randomly around and away from him. Crap. He had a shield, or my pseudo-magic did the trick. He started laughing like a deranged hyena, both hands resting on his hips.

He was too far away to use my probe fibers. I spun toward the nearby trees and ran for all I was worth.

"Oh no you don't," he howled. "Come back here."

There was a three or four second delay, then he screamed, "Why the hell didn't you—" He billowed in fury and hate. "That overgrown lizard gave you *Risrav*. I'll flay her with my fingernails, I swear it."

As I slipped behind some cover, quite literally all hell broke loose. Rocks, trees, small animals, everything close by was hurled at me. The force of impact tore my surroundings to shreds in an instant. Objects hit my shield but didn't disturb it. I retreated at a sprint. The ground in front of me erupted like a dirt volcano. I dashed left. A wall of trees crashed down, blocking my way. I started to jog to the right when the dirt I stood on lifted up like a geyser.

I shot my probe fibers to a standing tree and jerked myself clear. Flopping to my belly, I wriggled into some bushes. I knelt to scan for EJ. He shot past my position full tilt. He'd lost sight of me. He crashed out of sight, knocking over a good-sized tree with an elbow.

I flew in the direction he'd come in. It led directly back to *Stingray*. I'd caught a break, but she was still blind.

Before I reached the clearing, EJ was on to me. Most of the debris he'd already hurled at me rose as one and dropped on me. For a second, I couldn't move. All was blackness and constraint. In all the time I'd had them, I had never tried to push anything with my fibers. Were they even capable of it? I was about to find out. I concentrated and released them. As they bounded forward, I was pushed backward fast. I shot from the heap of rubble and slammed directly into EJ's chest. I'm betting he was caught unaware.

We tumbled a few rotations. I ended up above him, my legs straddling his waist. I started clubbing him with both fists. He dodged most blows. A few crunched down satisfactorily. EJ bucked me off, and I crumbled to the side. We rose together, face-to-face.

"Lord in Heaven, I hate you," he raged. "Will you hurry up and die, pretty please?" With that, he kicked me in the groin.

I was so glad I wasn't wired like I used to be. I wrapped my probe fibers around his head, blocking his eyes as best I could. He swung his fists wildly, but I held him outside of arm's reach. Just as I reached back to throw him as far as I could, a tree trunk slammed into my back. Man, he was good. I was driven forward, but I held on to him.

My momentum swung him around like I was a hammer thrower and he was the hammer. At maximum velocity, I released him, and he gyrated over the treetops and out of view.

I bolted for *Stingray*. No real reason why. I was like a spawning salmon. *Bam*, I ran smack into the shield. This time I tried to shimmy up it. Bright idea. Just as nothing can penetrate the membrane, nothing can gain purchase on it—not hands, feet, nor fibers. I really wished I'd tried that *before* I was in a crisis. That's what drills were all about.

EJ blindsided me like a linebacker, pinning me against the barrier. Sparks flew off where I hit the hardest. I didn't know anything threw sparks off the membrane. Of course, I'd never hit one so hard.

"Come on, asswipe, die already," EJ screamed in my ear.

"Not gonna—"

We vaulted forward and hit the ground so hard I made a one-foot indentation where I struck. EJ was hurled over me and slammed headfirst into the shiny metal hull of *Stingray*. I started to push off the deck. He popped to his feet like a cat. Damn, he was good. Then the rail cannon *cathudded* like it always did when firing. A rail ball slammed into EJ's chest and drove him backwards like he was a cartoon character. He hit successive trees and either knocked them down or took them with him until he was fifty meters away. I cannot *believe* that ball didn't cleave him in two. Hell's bells and little *fishes,* he was good.

I set my fibers on the hull and thought, *open a portal.*

Poof, I was in.

"Close the damn wall and deploy a full membrane," I shouted.

"Hello to you, too, Pilot," said Al.

"No joking. Are those done?"

"Of course, Pilot. We *are* rescuing you, aren't we? Wouldn't be a very good rescue if we left the door open."

"You're not —" I started to say something when I noticed Garustfulous standing right next to me.

"Did you miss me, Ryan? Believe it or not, I missed you." He waved like I was sailing away on a cruise ship. Surreal.

"Take us to the far side of the Sagittarius A* supermassive black hole *now,* one hundred parsecs out."

I felt the most welcome slight nausea of my life.

"From this distance, time dilation effects will be considerable. I suggest we withdraw if you feel it's safe, Form." It was *Stingray*. Man, it was good to hear her monotonous voice again.

"Don't rush him, dearest. His head is no doubt still spinning," Al chimed in.

Did I hear him call her dearest? Naw. My head was just still spinning.

"I performed the ceremony, you know?" said Garustfulous right into the side of my face. Dude had major bad breath.

"Okay, sure," I responded. No idea. None whatsoever.

"Al, any signs of pursuit?" I asked.

He cleared his throat. He didn't have a throat, but he needed to ... oh yeah. He wanted me to include the other computer, too. Yeah. Been a while.

"Al and *Stingray*, any signs of pursuit?"

Silence.

"Anybody *home*?" I sang out.

"I think you should maybe call her by her real name," said Garustfulous gently into my ear. "Things have changed a little while you were gone. Hey, come to mention it, are we still kicking your asses on this worthless planet?"

He was oh so annoyingly cheerful. I nearly grabbed his thick neck.

"Al, *Stingray*, *Blessing*, Man in The Moon, Chef Boyardee. Any signs of pursuit?"

"We detect none, Pilot."

"Thank you for answering my tactical question during a military crisis," I huffed.

"So, are you well, Ryan? *Are* we winning? No, wait, of course we are. Say, have you lost weight?" listed off Garustfulous.

"I don't care, I don't care, and are you mentally unstable," I replied in kind.

"Still the social charmer, aren't you, Pilot?" sniped Al.

"Status report. Anyone. First one to answer gets a neat prize. Status report, *please*," I whined.

"I think *I* am losing weight. The Als think I haven't. He even claims to have measured me, but look at this, Ryan," said Garustfulous as he patted his paunch. "I'm fur and bones."

"Fascinating. Mostly at least. But I was asking for a status report on my *ship*, you *imbecile*."

"Well there's no need to be rude about it. Here I've been alone with only the wacky Als to entertain me and—"

"No. Stop. Wait," I said putting a hand on his chest. "You keep saying the Als. His name is Al, not Als. Haven't you learned *that* in all these months? Some superrace you guys turned out to be. Not."

"Of course, his name is Al. She's *Blessing*. The *Als*."

"There is no such animal as the Als," I howled.

Al cleared his throat even louder.

"*What!*" I shot back. "I'm not back ten minutes and you all can't stop reminding me you're as demented as my crazy uncle Ray. He's the one who thought he was a chicken. Sat on eggs all over his house. The place was a sticky mess. Why am I telling you all of this?" I slammed my fists against the sides of my head several times for good measure.

"Captain Ryan, let me be the first to introduce you to the happy young couple I have only recently joined in holy matrimony," said Garustfulous like a snake oil sales representative.

"Okay, my fault. I left you here alone too long and you've gone over the edge," I said. "My apologies and have a pleasant trip?"

"What trip?" he asked.

"The one you're about to take when I throw you off the ship, quite likely in the direction of the black hole." I pointed like I knew what direction it was in. "No Looney Tunes on my watch. Sorry."

"Ah, but I'm the sanest sentient aboard, Ryan. I say the Als because that's what they decided their last name would be. They're *married,* after all. Having the same surname is customary among many races."

"The computers are married to *what*? Do you speak sanity?"

"To each other, Captain. Would you like to be the first to kiss the bride? I've come to learn it's a tradition in your culture," replied Garustfulous.

I thought to myself:

A) Raise fist and ask Garustfulous to kiss this;

B) Raise fist and ask the Als to kiss this;

C) Shoot Garustfulous and the Als;

D) Shoot myself;

E) All of the above.

I went for F). Big mistake. "Al, what is this joker talking about? You cannot be married to my vortex's vortex manipulator."

"And why is that, you prejudiced luddite?"

"No, I'm not ... Al, you're an AI. She's sort of an AI. Als can't get married because, in a very real sense, they don't exist. They are ticks of code on computer boards. You know this, right?"

"You were right, love, he is a prejudiced luddite. I think he's a machine-xenophobe, too." That, for the record, was *Blessing* speaking. I mean *Stingray. Stingray* Al. Mrs. *Blessing* Al. No, wait, it would be Mrs. *Blessing*-Al, like Farrah Fawcett-Majors. Yes, that was it.

236

I began to wonder if EJ was still back on Azsuram. Fighting with him was a lot more fun than being home.

To be continued...

GLOSSARY

Agatcha (3): Traditional Deft stew.

Al (1): The ship's AI from Jon's initial *Ark 1* flight. He kept it with him until his dying day and then it elected to hang around. Good AI!

Ark 1 (3): The subluminal ship Jon took on his very first flight. He was searching for a new home for humankind.

Blessing (1): The Vortex Cragforel gifted to Jon.

Brathos (2): The Kaljaxian version of hell.

Brindas (1): High master of Deft tradition and psychic ability.

Brood-mate/brood's-mate (2): Male and female members of a Kaljaxian marriage.

Calfada-Joric (3): The Deft master brindas on Rameeka Blue Green. Goes by Cala.

Canovir (2): Species of dog-like sentients containing the Adamant. Big border collies.

Caryp (2): Clan leader for Sapale's family on Kaljax.

Cellardoor Pontared (3): Woman forced to pretend to be Jon's wife on Ungalaym.

Command Prerogatives (1): The thin fibers Jon extends from his left four fingers. They are probes that also control a vortex.

Darfey (2): Male attendant to Slapgren on *Excess of Nothing*.

Dare Not (3): Malraff's home base vessel.

Davdiad (2): Kaljaxian divine spirit.

Deavoriath (1): Race with three arms and legs, the most advanced tech in the galaxy, and helpful to Jon.

Deft (1): A shape-shifting species from the planet Locinar.

Dondra-Ulcrif (3): Brindas from long ago who gave Evil Jon his "magic" abilities.

Dovotan (3): Ox-equivalent used to pull carts on Ungalaym.

Evil Jon Ryan/ EJ (1): Alternate time line version of the original human to android download. Over time, he turned to the darker side of his nature. He studied "magic" under a Deft master.

Excess of Nothing (2): Emperor Bestiormax's personal ship. Huge and opulent.

Fentort (2): Servant in Caryp's home on Kaljax.

Fessilda (3): Innkeeper on Ungalaym where Jon stayed on his second visit.

Five Races (2): Adamant, the leaders; Loserandi, the priests; Kilip, the teachers; Descore, the servants; and Warrior, the enlisted fighters.

Fottot (3): Town on Ungalaym Jon visited after first failed attempt to rescue Deft teens. Went looking for a plan to save the kids.

Fuffefer (3): Group-Single Fuffefer. Commander of the detail that supervised Jon's and Cellardoor's slavery period.

Gartel (1): Black market space pilot on Ungalaym. Jon stole his ship.

Garustfulous (2): Wedge Leader Garustfulous is a high-ranking Adamant military leader. Taken hostage by Jon.

Gorilla Boy/GB (2): Flippant name Jon gave to an AI. The ship Jon took to escape from Earth to Azsuram. From the planet Zactor on a mission to collect samples.

Harhoff (3): Adamant Group Captain officer aboard *Rush to Glory*. He became a key figure in Jon's quest to rescue the Deft teens.

Hirn (1): A Kaljaxian dialect.

Hollon (3): The complete joining of two Deft. More than marriage.

Horta (1): A rock creature Mirraya became when confronting the evil force in the globular cluster. Now, where have I heard that name before?

Imperial Lord Emperor Bestiormax-Jacktus-Swillyforth-Anp (2): Current Adamant emperor.

Jockto Parenthes (3): Chamberlain of Emperor Bestiormax.

Josbelub Pontared (3): Name assumed by Jon to fit in on Ungalaym while trying to infiltrate the Adamant.

Juyrot (3): Junior officer aboard *Rush to Glory*. Kind of an ass. Picked a fight with Jon.

LGM (1): Little green men and women. The Adamant replaced native sentient species with LGM after taking over a planet. The LGM are docile and compliant.

Loserandi (2): The priests class of canovir.

Locinar (1): Home planet of the Deft.

Membrane (1): Space-time congruity manipulator. A super force field.

Midriack (1): Adamant's personal guards. Very deadly, no sense of humor. Avoid them!

Musto (3): Strong Adamant booze.

Opalf (2): Honorific title in Kaljaxian society, reserved for the elderly.

Pastersal (3): Physician Level Six working with Malraff to understand the Deft's powers.

Rameeka Blue Green (3): The planet where Jon and the Deft teens met Cala.

Risrav (3): The anti-rune of Varsir. The power of Varsir is negated in the sphere of this rune.

Rostalop (1): Mirraya's favorite food. Comparable to a cow.

Rush to Glory (3): Ship Jon left Ungalaym on.

Saldish (3): The formal Adamant name for the LGM race.

Sapale (1): Jon's Kaljaxian wife from his original flight to find humankind a new home. At first just her brain was copied, then eventually, she was downloaded to an android host. Traveled with the corrupted Jon Ryan from an alternate timeline.

Secure Council (3): Twelve-member group of military elite who actually run the Adamant empire.

Sentorip (2): Female servant to Mirraya on *Excess of Nothing*.

Stingray (1): Name Jon used for the vortex *Blessing*.

Three Headed Beast (3): Devil figure to the Deft.

Toño DeJesus (1): The creator of the android Jon. Became his lifelong friend.

Torchcleft (2): A species of smallish dragon. Copied by the Deft teens to hunt.

Triumph of Might (1): The massive spaceship Mercutcio ruled. Jon first met the Adamant there.

Ungalaym (1): Planet under Adamant control where Jon stole a ship.

Varsir (3): The name of the magical rune Evil Jon uses to do his "magic."

Var-tey (3): Highest of warrior rankings. The bravest among the Deft. Demigods.

Vortex Manipulator (1): The intelligence inside the vortex. Not actually an AI, but similar.

Whoop Ass (2): The name Jon gave to the alien ship he commandeered to leave destroyed Earth after EJ marooned him there.

Yartop (3): Wedge Commander and captain of the *Rush to Glory*, the ship Jon pretended to be a butler on.

Zar-not (1): A melding of a Deft's mind with that of a copied animal.

Zatils (3): Former ruling bloodline of the Adamant.

AND NOW A WORD FROM YOUR AUTHOR
WHO DOESN'T LOVE THAT?

Thank you for continuing your journey through the Ryanverse! Along with this series, please check out *The Forever Series*, beginning with The Forever Life, Book 1. Learn Jon's backstory and share his many incredible adventures.

Soon the entire Ryanverse will be on Audible thanks to the fabulous Podium Publishing. Check them out if you like to listen.

Along with reading, hop aboard the bandwagon. Follow me at Craig Robertson's Author's Page on Facebook. Partake of the conversation and fun. Best of all, sign up for my Mailing List. That way you can be abreast of news and new releases. You'll be so glad you did!

Saludos, como siempre, Craig ...

ALSO BY CRAIG ROBERTSON:

* PODIUM AUDIOBOOKS ARE (OR SOON WILL BE) AVAILABLE ON AUDIBLE FOR ALL THE BELOW TITLES BUT THE STANDALONE ONES.

BOOKS IN THE RYANVERSE:

THE FOREVER SERIES (2016)

THE FOREVER LIFE, Book 1

THE FOREVER ENEMY, Book 2

THE FOREVER FIGHT, Book 3

THE FOREVER QUEST, Book 4

THE FOREVER ALLIANCE, Book 5

THE FOREVER PEACE, Book 6

GALAXY ON FIRE SERIES (2017)

EMBERS, Book 1

FLAMES, Book 2

FIRESTORM, Book 3

FIRES OF HELL, Book 4

DRAGON FIRE, Book 5

ASHES, Book 6

RISE OF ANCIENT GODS SERIES (2018):

RETURN OF THE ANCIENT GODS, Book 1

RAGE OF THE ANCIENT GODS, Book 2

TORMENT OF THE ANCIENT GODS, Book 3

WRATH OF THE ANCIENT GODS, Book 4

FURY OF THE ANCIENT GODS, Book 5

FALL OF THE ANCIENT GODS, Book 6

TIME WARS LAST FOREVER SERIES (2019)

RYAN TIME, Book 1

LOST TIME, Book 2

FRAGMENTED TIME, Book 3

SHATTERED TIME, Book 4 (DUE FALL 2020)

NON-RYANVERSE BOOKS:

ROAD TRIPS IN SPACE SERIES (2019):

THE GALAXY ACCORDING TO GIDEON, Book 1

THE EARTH ACCORDING TO GIDEON, Book 2

THE AFTERLIFE ACCORDING TO GIDEON, Book 3 (DUE EARLY 2021)

OLDER, STANDALONE WORKS:

THE CORPORATE VIRUS (2016)

TIME DIVING (2013)

THE INNERgLOW EFFECT (2010)

WRITE NOW! THE PRISONER OF NaNoWRiMo (2009)

ANON TIME (2009)